KATHERINE
A REGENCY ROMANCE

JENNY HAMBLY

BACHELOR BRIDES BOOK 3

DEDICATION

To Kate,
thank you for all those happy
hours we spent reading together!

ACKNOWLEDGMENTS

Thank you, Dave, for believing in me! Without your constant support and understanding I would not be following my dream.

Thanks go to Melanie Underwood for casting her eagle eyes over my words.

CHAPTER 1

A travelling carriage and a lone rider turned through the gates of Elmdon Hall and made their unhurried progress along the well-kept drive that was lined with the trees it was named after. The rider made no attempt to communicate with the occupants of the carriage, his bright blue eyes too busy drinking in every detail of the achingly familiar vista before him, as a man dying of thirst might view the sudden appearance of an oasis.

It had been five long years since Harry Treleven had seen his home and as the sun made a sudden appearance from behind the sullen grey clouds, the many small-paned windows of the Elizabethan manor began to wink brightly as if in welcome.

"Elmdon," he whispered, a slow wide grin transforming his unusually sombre countenance. Suddenly impatient to be within the portals of his home again, he touched his heels to his horse's flanks and encouraged the weary beast into one last gallop.

Elmdon Hall had been the principal home to the Trelevens for seven generations. It had first been gifted to Marcus Treleven, who had been a reckless but successful privateer and an annoying wasp to the Spanish, frequently intercepting their ships and filling Queen Elizabeth's coffers as well as lining his own pockets. She'd rewarded him with a knighthood and his son, a courtier to James I, was later awarded the title of viscount.

Perhaps it was this illustrious history that had tempted his descendent, the present viscount, to attempt such a lifestyle when he had been forced to flee the country after a duel over a lady that had left her husband, Lord Worthington, at death's door. That door had remained firmly closed however, and Lord Worthington had made a slow but steady recovery. It had only been when Harry had become dangerously ill with malaria and in serious danger of crossing that threshold himself, that he had discovered his mistake and returned to the shores of his birth.

This could not have been achieved without the aid of his good friend, Sir Philip Bray, who had travelled to Italy to bring him home and entered the state of connubial bliss soon afterwards. Indeed, it had been his nuptials that had delayed his return further.

The house was generally acknowledged to be a gracious building of pleasing proportions, the Trelevens not succumbing to the temptation that so frequently gripped their acquaintances, to add to their consequence by adding on wings that they could have little use for and more often than not, detracted from the handsomeness of the original building. Containing only ten principal bedrooms, it was not so large that a visitor might easily lose their way nor yet so compact that its occupants could never find a quiet corner in which to relax and contemplate their good fortune.

It sat in rolling parklands that spread in all directions as far as the eye could see, and although the park was mostly naturalistic in style, it still boasted an authentic knot garden and well-tended maze that dated back to the house's Tudor origins.

It took a good twenty minutes at least to arrive at the house once any visitor had passed through the gates, and much longer on foot, although as it sat on a small rise towards the centre of the park, it could be seen long before this.

The clattering of hooves on cobbles brought Kenver, the head groom at Elmdon, out of the stables. He was a small, wiry man with a weather-beaten face and a naturally taciturn disposition. He was not best pleased at being interrupted, as he had been busy mending one of the stall doors, which a bad tempered mare had kicked half off its hinges. He strode into the yard, his mallet still clutched in one fist and his annoyance writ large upon his dour countenance.

He stopped short when he saw his long absent master, dropped the mallet, and blinked rapidly as if to clear his vision. As Harry swung down from the saddle and strode towards him, he put his hands on his hips and let out a low whistle. For a moment it looked like Harry might actually embrace him and he thrust out a work-roughened hand to discourage such an unthinkable occurrence. However, he shook his hand warmly and the lines around his small, dark eyes deepened as a rare wide smile crept across his face.

"Lord Treleven," he said. "Welcome home, sir. Welcome home!"

Harry grinned. "Hello, Kenver, glad to see you, even if you do still look like you've lost a sovereign and found a farthing!"

"Is that so, sir? Well you may be right, but if you don't mind me saying so, you've turned into a right spindleshanks and no mistake. Best get yourself in to see Mrs Kemp, she'll soon put some meat on your bones!"

"I will, for I am famished. You can show me what cattle we have later, Kenver."

He shook his head ruefully. "The stable's not what it once was, sir."

"Not to worry, Kenver, not to worry, we'll soon sort that out!" the viscount assured him breezily, already striding towards the back of the house.

Mrs Kemp had been the cook at Elmdon ever since Harry could remember and a firm ally. Always active and usually hungry, he had been forever haunting the kitchens as a child, knowing she would give him something tasty to keep him going until dinnertime. She was busy pummelling some dough, with an energy that belied her age, when he entered the kitchen, and did not so much as glance up. Shutting the door behind him, he leant against it nonchalantly.

"What has taken you so long?" she snapped,

clearly mistaking him for one of the scullery maids.

"That is a long story, but I came as soon as I could, I assure you," he replied softly.

The pummelling stopped. Mrs Kemp's head whipped around, revealing a round rosy face and a satisfyingly startled expression.

"Master Harry! Master Harry!" she squealed, his boyishly cheeky grin causing her to slip into the form of address she had used when he was but a child. "Is it really you?"

Pushing himself away from the wall, he strode forwards and caught her up in a hug. "Mrs Kemp, Mrs Kemp!" he laughed. "It is indeed, me. A very famished me! Please say you have something to stop the infernal rumbles that have been issuing from my unruly stomach for the past hour and more!"

She emerged from his warm clasp, slightly flustered, with her cap askew and her eyes suspiciously bright.

"Now, that's enough of that, sir. You are the viscount now and need to remember your station *and mine*. It is most improper that you manhandle me in such a fashion! Or that you should creep in through the back door like a servant."

Harry hung his head as if in shame. "I must apologise, Mrs Kemp, I did not mean to wound your dignity, but I really am very hungry you know."

She was not fooled for an instant by his humble display. "Oh, sit down, Lord Treleven, do. I don't know what you've been up to or where you've been but there is nothing to you, and that's the truth! But don't you worry none, we'll soon have you fattened up!" Disappearing for a moment into a small adjacent pantry, she re-emerged with a jug of ale and a plate of cakes.

"Here you are, sir, get this down you for starters!"

"Mrs Kemp, Mrs Kemp!" This time the refrain came from the inner corridor. "Lady Treleven's carriage is coming up the driveway. Why she didn't write to warn us, I don't know!"

The door opened on these words to reveal the harassed looking housekeeper. Harry's back was towards her, so all she saw was a strange man wolfing down cakes.

"Who is this?" she said sternly. "This is not the time to be feeding all and sundry, Mrs Kemp, not with her ladyship being almost at the door!"

Harry hastily swallowed, took a swig of ale, and turned to greet the newcomer. "Have you already forgotten me, Biddy?" he twinkled.

No one else would have dared address Mrs Bidulph, a very correct housekeeper, in such a fashion. She pressed her hands over her heart as she gasped, "Lord Treleven? Can it be you?"

Pushing himself to his feet, he took both her hands in his own and dropped a swift kiss on her pale cheek. "Indeed it can. Now bustle about, Biddy, you must go and greet mother, remember."

"Of course, sir," she said, pulling herself together. She paused at the door as if something had just occurred to her. Turning back she said, "Will you be changing rooms, my lord?"

A shadow seemed to flit across Harry's face. "No, my own room will do nicely for now."

Nodding briskly, she bustled out, all business again.

Word about Viscount Treleven's return soon got out in the mysterious way these things do in the country and it was not long before a stream of visitors made their way to Elmdon. Families who had long since given up trying to engage with Lady Treleven, who had become quite reclusive after the disappearance of her son followed shortly after by the death of her beloved husband in an unfortunate riding accident, now made a concerted effort to renew their acquaintance; especially if they had daughters of marriageable age.

They found Lady Treleven quite transformed and even her shy daughter Henrietta, slightly less awkward than before. Although this was generally viewed as a welcome development, more than one ambitious mother found herself disappointed, for Lord Treleven proved annoyingly elusive during these frequent visits.

This was only partly due to him throwing himself into learning the business of running his estate, something he did with great energy and application; he had never been one to do anything by halves, but also because he had made it crystal clear to Glasson, his butler, that he expected him to pronounce him 'not at home' if anyone arrived with their daughters in tow.

This instruction had not been issued because he held females in contempt, far from it, he had always had an eye for the ladies, but he preferred to further any acquaintance on his own terms and avoided matchmaking mamas like the plague. Although he was pleased that his friend Philip had finally found his life's partner, he had no intention of following his example any time soon. He was fairly certain he would be the devil of a husband! Not one to deny his own weaknesses, he knew he had a roving eye and had never yet met a woman he had not wearied of within a sennight.

At the present time, he preferred to re-acquaint himself with his country. His estate was on the north coast of Cornwall and it ran all the way to the wide expanse of sea that bordered the county.

It was here that he had ventured today, escaping both visitors and his steward. Mr Hewel was honest enough and had served the family, like most of their servants, for a long time, however he was not as young as he once was and Harry feared he had quite exhausted him as he had endeavoured to acquire as much information as possible in a relatively short time. His estate was huge and he had not yet surveyed above half of it, but it was already clear to him that much needed to be done. Mr Hewel had fallen behind the times and no new investments or innovations had been attempted for some years. He should perhaps pension him off, but he sensed that Mr Hewel was not yet ready for an idle life and he would not repay loyal service in such a way.

A warm wind buffeted him as he approached the cliff, and he took a long breath inhaling deep the fresh sea air, tasting the salty tang upon his tongue. The recent rains had encouraged a riot of growth and a luxuriant carpet spread before him, embroidered with splashes of blue, white, pink and yellow as sea campion, thrift, stonecrop and alexanders threaded their way through it. He picked his way carefully towards the cliff edge, wary lest the growth hid a rabbit hole or two.

Allowing his mount to drop his head and enjoy the small, yellow flowers of the alexanders, he let his eyes rove over the wide expanse before him. The choppy grey-green waters were flecked with angry flurries of white foam which scornfully burst over or rushed around the dark rocks which stood like silent giants, barring entry to the clean, empty stretch of golden sand beyond. Above gulls wheeled and gannets dived, their raucous calls striking a discordant note above the ever present rumble of the crashing surf.

By God, he had missed this country! It spoke to something deep within him, stripping from him all artifice and calling to his most primitive self. If the day had been calmer he would have been tempted to make his way down the narrow path that wound towards the beach below and dive into those cold, clear waters, and celebrate his homecoming with a baptismal swim. It would be foolhardy today however, as not only was the sea rough, but from his vantage point he could clearly see the white and brown rush as waves and sand were sucked under and dragged out again by a strong current.

Only a fool would underestimate the sea; beneath those waves lay the wrecks and bones of many ships and sailors who had come to grief on this treacherous stretch of coast. Shaking off this melancholy thought, he turned his horse and made his way back to the cliff path. He could see the tall granite chimney and engine house of Wheal Trewith in the distance. Although the mines offered much needed employment to the local people, he could not help but think they were a blight on this naturally wild and beautiful landscape.

He knew that Lord Trewith had at one time suggested his father invest and even that they explore the possibilities of tunnelling into his own land, but he could not say he was sorry that the idea had come to naught. He would much rather invest in farming the land, providing jobs and much needed sustenance rather than plunder it for its natural resources. He was however, going to have to expand his interests sooner or later; a combination of poor harvests and a drop in the price of crops had seriously undermined the productivity of the land, eating not only into his own profits but those of his tenant farmers.

Lord Trewith, like his own father, was no longer of this earth and his son, not sharing his head for business or love of the West Country, which he had been known to refer to as a social wasteland, had sold the estate whilst he had been away. He had not yet met Mr Caldwell, the current owner and his nearest neighbour of any note, but no doubt he would soon enough. He could only give him credit for giving him time to settle in before paying his visit and could wish that a few others had shown such forethought.

He turned away from the mine and headed towards the village of Langarne. The ride had given him a thirst and if his memory served him correctly, The Anchor served a decent brew. It had also used to boast a very cosy armful who went by the name of Mollie Penrose.

Langarne was reached down a long, winding, steep lane. Tall hedges and towering trees threw it almost constantly into shifting shadow and in winter it could be treacherous. At the bottom of the hill, the village spread out along the banks of a river, made up of mostly small thatched cottages, the inn, and a church and vicarage, which stood slightly apart across a small green. Other than a few women washing clothes down by the river, and an old man sunning himself outside his cottage, sucking on his pipe, it was largely deserted today. The man nodded at Harry as he passed.

"Glad to see you back, Lord Treleven, and not before time, if I may say so," he said, removing the pipe from his mouth. "Things go to ruin when those as knows the land and its people leave it be."

Harry gave him an intent stare, vaguely aware of currents flowing beneath his words that he could not quite navigate.

"Well, I am back now, my good man, and I will do my best to set it in order, you may be sure."

The wizened old man regarded him just as closely for a moment and then nodded, put his pipe back in his mouth, and spoke around the obstruction. "Happen you will, sir, happen you will."

A young lad came running as he turned into the yard of The Anchor. Harry dismounted, tossed a coin to the boy and strode into the inn. It was a warren of small rooms, with low beams and flagged floors, and he was surprised to see sullen men who should have been out earning a crust, occupied more than one.

"Lord Treleven!" beamed a tall, spare man

with a thatch of dark hair, putting down the cloth he had been wiping the bar with. "I heard as you were back and was wondering how long it would be before you paid us a visit. I told Mollie as how you wouldn't think yourself too high and mighty just because you have a title now!"

Harry grinned and shook the huge hand offered to him. "I should think not, Joe. I have been looking forward to a tankard of your fine ale. Is old Jack about?"

Joe shook his head and began pouring his ale. "M'father died of pneumonia last winter, sir. I run the place now."

"Oh, do you now, Joe Phelps? We'll soon see about that!"

"Mollie!" Harry roared, his eyes lighting with laughter. Spinning around he lifted the curvaceous red-haired woman who stood before him, her hands on her nicely rounded hips, clean off of her feet, twirling her around before planting a brief kiss on her smiling lips.

"Put me down, Harry, do, afore you drop me. I don't know what mischief you've been up to but you're thin as a cord. There was obviously no decent food to be had on whatever godforsaken shore you washed up on!"

"Ahem." The noise was quietly made, but

they both glanced over to see Joe observing them, a small frown furrowing his broad brow.

"No offence, Lord Treleven, sir, but I would rather you weren't quite so familiar with my wife," he said, his voice gentle but quite firm.

Harry took a step back as Mollie flushed slightly. "You're married, Mollie?"

"She is that," confirmed Joe seriously. "And I would remind you, Mollie, that what is past is past and best forgotten and as his lordship has come into his title, an all, you should address him as Lord Treleven from now on."

Mollie's rueful eyes might have held a smidgeon of regret but she curtsied briefly to Harry. "Joe's right enough, everything is different now, H-my lord, we was wed last year and I have never been happier."

Harry's smile was a little lopsided. "I am pleased for you both," he assured them glancing around the room, suddenly aware of more than one pair of resentful eyes upon him.

"Why aren't these men out working?" he asked quietly.

Joe lowered his voice and leant in a little closer. "You'd be better asking Mr Caldwell the answer to that, sir, he's a deep 'un and proud as Lucifer. A lot of things have changed, my lord, and not for the better neither."

"Go on," Harry murmured.

"Seems he wasn't satisfied with Cornish miners who were born and bred to the trade. Brought a load over from Wales along with his coal, and on the last setting day they bid so low, they were awarded the contracts. There's a lot of bad feeling round here and no mistake and I wouldn't be surprised if there was trouble afore long. A few have got work in the boatyards at Padstow, the rest sits in here, nursing their resentment over a drink they can't afford and will likely never pay for."

"I see," Harry said frowning. "I will indeed ask Mr Caldwell for his reasons, Joe, of that you can be sure. Meanwhile, I'll have a word with Mr Hewel and my mother, it may be that we could do with some extra help."

Joe nodded tersely. "I 'as always said you were a good 'un, honest as the day is long."

Leaving his horse at The Anchor, Harry strode across the village green towards the vicarage. A few women had just come from there, and passed him with their eyes downcast, the aroma of freshly baked bread wafting from their cloth covered baskets.

A squat housekeeper with a fierce beetle-black glare opened the door, her expression as sour as curdled milk.

"I've no more bread to—"

Harry grinned at her. "What about one of your biscuits, Mrs Creedley?"

Harry had been sent down from Oxford on more than one occasion, and his father, though secretly admiring his pluck, had insisted he spent some of the time studying with the Reverend James Gulworthy, a widower, who had the reputation of being something of a scholar.

"Lord Treleven! The prodigal son returns, at last. You'd best come in," she sniffed, "as if I haven't got enough to do with looking after the vicar and the new doctor, as well as feeding half the village!"

Not at all put out by the lack of ceremony with which she greeted him, Harry followed her down the dark, panelled hallway into the large kitchen. She went to a covered plate that sat on the scrubbed wooden side and plonked it none too gently on the large pine table that ran almost the length of the kitchen, then stood glaring at him with folded arms.

Glancing out of the window, Harry saw the balding pate of Mr Gulworthy bent over a small rose bush. Mrs Creedley followed his gaze.

"He'd be better tending his flock than his precious roses! If he were one of those methody preachers he'd be turning them out of The Anchor and giving them a lecture on the evils of drinking. Instead he preaches about how the bountiful eye shall be blessed for giving his bread to the poor, and I'm the fool that has to make it!"

Harry glanced at the housekeeper, surprised. She might appear curmudgeonly but he knew that she had a good heart and he had never before heard her berate her absentminded master.

"And you needn't stand there looking down your nose, neither. You're no better!"

Harry felt himself stiffen, his eyes hardening. Mrs Creedley suddenly burst into tears.

"I'm sorry, my lord. I didn't mean it, but everything's topsy-turvy round here at the moment."

Flicking back the cloth that covered the plate, he took a biscuit and laid a hand briefly on her shaking shoulder.

"Calm yourself, Mrs Creedley, you may be sure I will look into matters here."

The afflicted lady rummaged for a handkerchief in her apron pocket and promptly wiped her eyes and blew her nose.

"I know you will, sir, you always were a good boy, really."

Mr Gulworthy glanced up as Harry approached, unhurriedly finished deadheading a few more roses, then smiled and held out his hand.

"Lord Treleven. Welcome home, sir, welcome home. Your return is the best news we have had in these parts for some time."

"That is not a view shared by all, I think," he replied a little grimly.

Mr Gulworthy shook his head. "Things are not as they once were, Lord Treleven. The villagers feel let down, abandoned, hopeless and bitter."

Harry sighed. "Mrs Creedley also seems deeply affected."

"Yes, well, her favourite nephew has just sailed from Padstow for America, hoping to find a better life, so we must forgive her if she is a little more crotchety than usual."

Harry frowned. "Have you had any dealings with Mr Caldwell?"

The vicar's gentle gaze hardened. He turned back to his flowers and firmly snipped the wilting head of another fading rose.

"I reminded him of proverbs 22:1," he assured him.

Harry raised a quizzical brow.

The vicar sighed. "You never were one to stick to your books. 'A good name is rather to be chosen than great riches, and loving favour rather than silver and gold'."

"And his response?"

"The heathen laughed in my face," he said gravely.

CHAPTER 2

Miss Katherine Lockhart stretched weary limbs and sighed. She had been on the road for almost a week but it felt like forever. Her brother, Sir Richard Lockhart, had informed her that the ways into Cornwall were much improved in recent years, but if this were so, she shuddered to think what they had been like before. If it remained dry they had to negotiate ruts and dips that jolted all occupants of the carriage mercilessly – and no matter how stuffy and hot it became they were forced to keep the windows shut to prevent the dust from choking them – but if it came on to rain the road became a treacherous quagmire in a matter of moments. It was perhaps these indis- putable facts that had discouraged her brother from making the journey himself when a distant relation he had never met had unexpectedly bequeathed him his property, Helagon, more than a year ago. His solicitor had informed him that it was a modest house in quite an isolated spot and might benefit from some slight renovation. It was to this property that Katherine was now making her plodding way.

She had really been left with very little choice. She had only once met someone she had felt the slightest tendre for and he had turned out to be a sad disappointment. Having a natural inclination to manage, she had been happy enough running Sir Richard's elegant house for him, but it could not be contemplated that she could continue to do so as he had recently been married. His wife, Caroline, understandably wanted to put her own mark on Felsham Court, and this was not always easy when the servants were used to the way Miss Lockhart ordered things. When, exasperated, Caroline had suggested it might be time to replace some of them, Katherine had realised that her continued presence was quite untenable. Unwilling to see any loyal retainers turned off or to remain a drain on her brother's resources when she no longer held any useful role within his household – and having no considerable fortune of her own – she had suggested she look about her for a post as governess or companion.

Sir Richard had looked horrified, but fully aware that the continued presence of both women under his own roof would inevitably disturb his peace, had offered her a compromise; she would travel to Helagon and put it in order, and if she liked it there, she could have its use for as long as she wished. Despite her four and twenty years, he had insisted she take a companion. Mrs Abbott was some sort of distant cousin to their departed mother and lived in a small cottage on his estate. She had been more than happy to accompany Katherine, delighted to feel that she was needed and could finally be of some real use.

And so they had set out on this interminable journey. Their slow progress was not due to the poor state of the highways alone however; if her brother had been prepared to lend them his best carriage and horses, they might have been much more comfortable and made swifter progress, but as Caroline had assured him that she could not do without it, that had not been an option.

"I am sure Katherine cannot mind taking the other coach, dear, for she is not in a hurry after all," she had said winningly, serving up the smile she reserved only for him. "And I really cannot be expected to be jolted about by that horrid rickety old thing in my present delicate condition."

Sir Richard's strong sense of decorum had not allowed him to entertain, even for a moment, the idea that his sister should make use of any form of public transport, and his penny-pinching ways had encouraged him to take notice of his wife when she had pooh-poohed the notion that they should hire a private post-chaise and four to convey his sister to her destination.

"It is such a shocking expense!" she had exclaimed. "And you have already been so very generous in gifting dear Katherine the use of Helagon for as long as she wishes. Although I hope I value my sister-in-law as I should, I am sure that it would cause her much discomfort to think that she had been such a burden to you, Richard. Do not forget that she will have the benefit of an experienced coachman who has known her all his life and if it *is* a little slow, that cannot signify for she will have the benefit of Mrs Abbott to keep her company."

That part was at least true. Mrs Abbott was perhaps not the brightest penny in the purse, but she had a good heart and a sweet disposition and Katherine found this refreshing after fielding Caroline's barely veiled barbs for the past six months.

Katherine turned her gaze to the open land-scape beyond the window of the carriage, it appeared to stretch endlessly before her and was quite alien in its character. It was a rough hardy terrain, strewn with large grey boulders and scrubby brush, but here and there bright bursts of yellow gorse or purple heather relieved the monotony. The huge sky cast an ominous feel over the whole, bruised lowering clouds stretched almost to the wide horizon and beneath them a fiery orb of molten gold threw its munificent soothing rays over strange outcrops of granite and stunted withered trees, which leaned towards it as if in silent supplication. It was a far cry indeed from the fertile, gently rolling hills near her own home, yet she felt herself somehow moved by the ancient unadorned scene before her.

Slowly the prospect gentled, the land showing signs of cultivation, and they descended into a deep wooded valley.

"It cannot be much further," Katherine murmured as they turned into a road so narrow that the twigs of untended bushes and trees scratched the sides of the lurching coach like skeletal fingers.

"I do hope not, dear," said Mrs Abbott a trifle anxiously, "for it is almost dark."

"It's an ungodly place if you ask me," muttered the other occupant of the carriage. "It wouldn't surprise me if there were hobgoblins out there."

Mrs Abbott looked a little alarmed.

Katherine favoured her maid with a stony stare. Caroline had recommended her, and wishing to avoid any unnecessary unpleasantness, she had agreed to give her a trial. Her disposition was surly however, and Katherine would have been tempted to replace her if she had had the time. But although she had resigned herself to tolerating her sour disposition, she would not countenance her upsetting Mrs Abbott.

"I do not believe anyone did ask you, Ayles, and if you cannot keep your tongue between your teeth, you shall ride on the roof next to coachman John."

Ayles bowed her head as if in deference, but Katherine noticed the sulky pout that she could not quite hide.

Dusk came on quickly and the dense woodland that bordered the road on either side intensified the gloom. The ladies were aware of a feeling of relief as they heard the crunch of gravel beneath them and realised they had turned into a driveway. As they descended from the carriage a sliver of moon appeared between the shifting clouds, casting its silvery light over the granite house in front of them, bathing it in a ghostly glow. No welcoming flicker from a fire or candle could be discerned behind any of the dark blank windows that seemed to stare blindly down at them.

Signalling for coachman John to stay where he was, Katherine stepped forwards and pulled the large iron bell that hung by the front door. It had clearly not been oiled for some time and squealed its protest at being thus awoken. The flapping of wings could be heard above its low sonorous chimes as roosting birds were disturbed, adding their disgruntled cries to the cool night air, and somewhere in the distance the mournful hoot of an owl completed the eerie atmosphere. Katherine shivered and pulled her cloak closer around her, at the same time silently castigating herself as a witless widgeon. She had always prided herself on her calm good sense and reason and here she was behaving more like her namesake Catherine Morland in Northanger Abbey! A novel she had not managed to finish as, although she could admire the wit of its writer, she was less able to bear with the overactive imagination of the heroine.

Nevertheless, she was grateful when a few moments later, a stooped, elderly gentleman who looked as if he should have been retired a long time since, opened the door. He attempted an unsteady bow and almost toppled forwards. Katherine automatically put out her hand to steady him and offered him a small smile.

"Good evening, I am Miss Lockhart, I do hope you were expecting us?" She glanced past him uncertainly into the dark panelled hallway.

"Forster, ma'am," he said, standing aside to let them pass. "We knew you were coming, Miss Lockhart, but were not sure exactly when to expect you."

Katherine was relieved. For a moment she had wondered if they had come to the wrong house and the awful prospect of resuming their journey had loomed before her. "I can see that," she said drily as she looked about the hallway. Even in the light of his flickering candle she could see that the wooden floors were dull and the table that stood at the base of the staircase, covered in a film of dust. Her housewifely instincts were revolted but she refrained from comment.

A little more light was shed upon this rather

dismal scene as a door at the end of the corridor burst open and a short, stout lady hurried forwards.

"Oh my, oh my," she said in a worried voice. "Miss Lockhart, I only had the letter two days ago and as there is only me and Forster left, everything is not yet as I would like, or at least as good as I could make it."

"There are only the two of you?" Katherine said, surprised.

The agitated lady before her nodded. "We had a maid or two and a gardener when Mr Jenkins was alive, but after he died they bailed. Said they weren't staying around in this gloomy place with no guarantee of getting paid anytime soon."

"Well, I must thank you, Mrs…?"

"Mrs Nance, ma'am."

"Mrs Nance and Forster for at least staying," she continued. "It is an unfortunate circumstance to be sure, but I am sure there will be no great difficulty in hiring a few more servants. But we can discuss what is to be done in the morning. Now, is there any chance of a fire and some supper?"

"I will go and lay the fire directly, ma'am," said Forster.

"Wait," said Katherine, thinking better of it. "Is there a fire in the kitchen, Mrs Nance?"

"There is indeed, ma'am."

"Good," Katherine said decisively. "We will take our supper there. We only require some tea and perhaps some cold meat and bread and butter before we retire."

"As you wish, ma'am, I have at least prepared the bedchambers and a room over the stables for your coachman."

She found things much more to her liking in the kitchen. A cheery fire burnt in the hearth, its flickering flames reflected in the gleaming copper pans that lined the walls and the table on which Mrs Nance laid their simple repast, was scrubbed spotlessly clean. Once they had eaten their fill, the housekeeper showed them to their rooms.

As they ascended to the first floor, many of the stairs creaking beneath them, Katherine shivered. A cold damp seemed to penetrate through the very stones of the house.

Her chamber was of a comfortable size, and apart from a bed hung with red velvet drapes that may have at one time been quite luxurious but were now sadly faded, it boasted a small threadbare armchair that was set before the empty fireplace, a washstand, a large armoire, a squat ugly dresser made of a dark wood and a toilet table upon which sat a slightly hazed mirror. Crossing to the window, Katherine firmly closed the worn curtains against the flickering shadows cast by the trees, which somehow rendered even the most ordinary items of furniture slightly menacing, blew out her candle, and climbed into bed. Her sheets were cool and un-welcoming but even this inconvenience could not keep her tired eyes from closing almost immedi-ately. Her last cogent thought before she fell into a deep slumber was that she was sure everything would seem much better in the morning.

When she opened her eyes, the first thing she saw was a nasty crack running across the ceiling above her. Sighing, she sat up. Mrs Nance had thoughtfully placed a small silver bell by her bedside and she rang it. The sooner she was up, the sooner she could assess the magnitude of the task she had undertaken.

Ayles eventually answered the summons on the third ring. Her eyes bore witness to her rest-less night, purple shadows and swollen eyelids a testament to her fitful sleep and her downturned mouth a clear indication of her feelings.

"Is everything all right, Ayles?" Katherine asked gently.

Her maid pursed her thin lips. "Oh, I've

nothing to complain about, Miss Lockhart. I daresay I will become quite used to mice running across my bed during the night, not to mention the branches of a tree scraping against my window, and I am not one to moan about the wind howling around the house as if a demented lost soul was trying to find its way in."

"I am sorry that your rest was disturbed, Ayles," she said, not unsympathetically. "But every house has its own foibles after all, and whilst I can do nothing about the wind, I am sure we can remedy the other annoyances."

Not wishing to put Mrs Nance to the blush, after breakfast she and Mrs Abbott made their own tour of the house. It was to be expected that after lying empty for some time it should bear an air of neglect, but judging by her growing list of problems, she could only imagine that their distant relative, Mr Jenkins, had been too tight-fisted to spend any money on its upkeep. He had certainly not been constrained by poverty for he had also left her brother quite a tidy sum, which he had begrudgingly put at her disposal to carry out whatever improvements were needed to make the house habitable.

"And if you don't like it, Katherine, once you have put it in order, you must come straight back," he had advised her, his sense of duty overcoming his dislike of being made uncomfortable. He was also fully aware that she had always managed his house extremely well on a modest budget, and had cast a wary eye over all the improvements that his new wife felt were necessary to her comfort. "I am certain it is Caroline's condition that is making her so crotchety, but once the child is born I am sure she will be only too grateful for some extra help with everything."

Katherine had repressed a shudder at this ingenuous speech, the implications of the word 'everything' conjuring up visions of herself dwindling into a maiden aunt who would be expected to fetch and carry for a never satisfied Caroline, or take care of her offspring when she inevitably discovered that the expense of a nursemaid was really not to be thought of when *dear* Katherine could have nothing better to do. She had determined there and then, that whatever she found awaiting her, she would make the best of it. However, she had certainly not expected Helagon to be quite so rundown.

"Might benefit from some slight renovation?" she muttered, not for the first time as they came upon yet another room with moth-eaten furnishings. She was, by now, expecting the patches of damp and windows that rattled in their frames rendering the simple act of keeping the draught out, quite impossible. Worse was to come, for two ceilings had partially collapsed in the servants' quarters and some of the floorboards were quite rotten.

Katherine was not one to make a drama out of a crisis, but felt her spirits sink at this scene of devastation. "It seems Richard's solicitor has quite a talent for understatement," she said grimly.

Mrs Abbott looked worried. "Perhaps it has deteriorated greatly over the last year?" she said, giving him the benefit of the doubt. "But, Katherine, dear, I do not see how we can expect to hire any more maids when we have nowhere for them to sleep."

"There can be no question of it," she agreed. "I presume the problem is with the roof, the tiles have probably slipped. Let us go into the garden and see."

They found the back of the house covered in climbing ivy, and the garden predictably dishevelled and neglected. A weed-choked path was just visible beneath the long, unkempt grass and they made their way along it as best they could in order to attain a better view of the house.

"Oh, Katherine, come over here, dear."

Turning her head, she saw that Mrs Abbott

had wandered off the path into the jungle beyond. She found her struggling to hold back the grass in order to take a closer look at something.

"Let me help," Katherine said, pulling back another section of undergrowth.

"Be careful, dear," Mrs Abbott warned. "There are some nasty brambles hidden in there."

It was a small but perfectly formed fountain, with a cherub standing on a plinth in the centre. Its mouth was pursed and in the absence of any water issuing from it, the winged child had an air of being surprised at the disturbance.

"It is a sign, my dear," Mrs Abbott said gently. "Everything will work out for the best, you wait and see. I think this garden could be quite lovely underneath this riot of grass and weeds."

Despite herself, Katherine smiled. Mrs Abbott was a keen gardener and had lovingly tended her own small patch of garden at Felsham. Her optimistic words strengthened Katherine's resolve; if Mrs Abbott could see through this wilderness to the potential that lay beneath, then she must do the same with the house.

She could clearly see now where some tiles had slipped and others had been blown clean off the roof. Plants had already started to take their place, but taking Mrs Abbott's lead she tried to look at the house with new eyes. It was larger than she had expected and not unpleasing in its proportions. Once the ivy had been stripped away and some of the trees that grew too close to the building, chopped down, it would look quite attractive. She would have to throw an army of workmen both into the house and garden, but it could be done.

The small stables that were set a little back at the side of the house were sheltered from the prevailing wind by a stand of trees, and were not as dilapidated as she had feared. Apart from her own carriage, there was a rather forlorn gig covered in dust but apparently still in one piece.

"All's well, John?" she asked her coachman, who was busy sweeping the floor.

"I've seen worse, ma'am," he said gruffly, "but I'll be needing some help if you want things set to rights anytime soon."

"I will set about getting some help immediately," she assured him. "But in the meantime you are only to do what is necessary to make your own living arrangements more comfortable."

Mrs Nance looked up a little anxiously as they entered the kitchen and she reassured her with a calm smile.

"Mrs Nance, I am all admiration. I cannot imagine how you and Forster have managed in such a ramshackle place."

"Well, miss, it wasn't always as bad as this. But if you don't mind me talking frankly about a relation of yours, Mr Jenkins was not one to spend a penny when a ha'penny would do. He became quite eccentric in his last years; lived and slept in his library and ignored the rest of the house. I expect as you'll be off now you've seen it for yourself." Her tone was resigned and she bowed her head. "I don't know what's to happen to old Forster and me."

"Well I can tell you, Mrs Nance," Katherine said firmly. "You are going to be very busy presently, for we are going to turn this place about. I think this house could be quite charming with a little restoration and Mrs Abbott and I have already agreed that the garden will be delightful."

When Mrs Nance raised her head, her face was wet with tears. "It's what I've always said, miss, it's wrung my heart to see such a fine residence turn to wrack and ruin so it has."

Mrs Abbott took her arm and led her to the table.

"There, dear, sit down and rest for a moment. I'll make you a reviving cup of tea. You'll need all your strength presently for you'll have an army of hungry mouths to feed."

Mrs Nance revived at the very thought and stepped away from the table.

"That's as music to my ears, Mrs Abbott, but I'll not have you waiting on me, it's not fitting. We'll have a cup of tea but I shall make it."

"I am going to need a little advice on how best to proceed," Katherine said thoughtfully. "Where do you suggest I seek it?"

"There's only one place near here where I think you'll get any useful sort of advice, and that'll be at Elmdon Hall, ma'am. The Trelevens have farmed the country around here for gen-erations."

Katherine nodded decisively. "Well, then it is to Elmdon Hall I shall go, and there is no time like the present."

CHAPTER 3

Katherine's suggestion that she drive herself in the gig did not go down well with coachman John, who had had the privilege of teaching Katherine to both ride and drive and so did not hesitate to speak his mind.

"Now don't be hasty, ma'am," he said in his unhurried way. "It's not that I question your ability to drive it, you're a fine whip and do me credit, but what I do doubt is its ability to be driven. That gig has not been used for years and will need a proper looking at before it can be deemed serviceable, like everything else around here. Besides, you can't take it before you get a groom, for I'll not try and squeeze these old bones into a seat that is only fit for a lad, and if you think Sir Richard would thank me if I was to let you go haring about this countryside on your own, you've got windmills in your head. It won't take me many minutes to get the carriage ready, she's a fine old gal for a short journey, after all."

Katherine had had no thought of asking him to accompany her, only wishing to allow him a rest after their tiring journey, but she supposed she should have known better; coachman John took his duties very seriously.

Although there was still a strong breeze blowing, the day was fair, white puffs of cloud chased each other across an azure sky and the narrow lanes seemed far less daunting when bathed in glorious sunshine. Once out of the valley, the trees marched in ordered lines along the hedgerows and the warm air shimmered with birdsong. Relaxing back against the squabs of her seat, Katherine allowed her mind to wander as her eyes roamed over the tranquil rural scene.

As they approached the wide gateway of the Elmdon estate, a deer ran across the road in front of them. The carriage had already slowed to turn into the drive so neither the graceful creature or the horses were much alarmed by this event – but the short explosive crack that snapped through the air moments later had them jibbing in their bits.

Startled, Katherine pushed down her window and leaned out. "John?" she called.

"Don't you go fretting, ma'am," he said, with his usual calm. "It'll be some gentleman or other after a pheasant or two, I'll be bound."

They had not gone many yards into the park however, when they saw someone stagger to his feet clutching his arm and a riderless horse tearing down the avenue. Barely waiting for the carriage to come to a halt, Katherine jumped down into the road. Brushing down her skirts she turned to the stranger.

"Sir, you are hurt, can I be of some assistance?" she asked, her cool tone at variance with her impetuous action.

Harry offered her a small bow and a rueful smile. "It is nothing, ma'am, a mere scratch. I have suffered much worse I assure you and have had some practise at being thrown from horses."

"Then you have either been most unfortunate or very careless, sir," Katherine said, her small smile taking any sting from her words. "But please, allow me to bind your arm and take you up to the house."

"It is quite unnecessary," he insisted.

Katherine's clear hazel eyes dropped pointedly to the glistening dark red stain that had ruined his coat.

"Come now, sir, if it is only a scratch then it will not hurt very much to get that coat off you, and if it is of a more serious nature, the sooner we remove it the better, for you do not wish any stray threads to get into the wound."

Her patient, reasonable tone was very much in the style of a nurse re-assuring a recalcitrant child.

"I thought any lady worth the name was meant to faint at the sight of blood," Harry murmured provocatively.

Katherine merely raised a haughty brow leaving him in no doubt at all that she was every inch a lady. Before he could argue further, John was behind him, helping ease the tight fitting coat over his shoulders.

"Best do as you're told, sir," he said encouragingly as Harry winced. "Miss Lockhart is in the right of it."

Once the coat was removed, Katherine took a step forwards. She had retrieved a small pair of scissors from her reticule and began to snip at the material around the wound in an efficient manner.

"I have been a keen supporter of the infirmary in Bath," she informed him conversationally. "I discovered I have quite an interest in medical matters, and have frequently observed the surgeons there treat a variety of wounds."

"Really? And that makes you an expert, I suppose," Harry said, eyeing her scissors warily.

"No," Katherine replied unruffled, "just an enthusiastic amateur."

In a matter of moments the wound was laid bare and Katherine bent closer to observe it more closely.

Straightening she smiled sweetly at him. "I would not call it a mere scratch, sir. It runs quite deep and is bleeding quite profusely at the moment but it is not, I think, too serious. Have you a flask of brandy about you?"

"No, Miss Lockhart, I do not." Annoyed at her interference, Harry was terse. "I am not in the habit of imbibing spirits every time I take a ride."

If he had thought to wrong-foot her, he was sadly mistaken.

"I am glad to hear it, sir, but as you seem so accident prone it occurred to me that you might have become accustomed to carrying one to fortify yourself whenever you were thrown."

A glimmer of appreciation shone in the

bright eyes that were suddenly closely regarding her and an appealing dimple was revealed as his lips reluctantly twitched into a grin. For the first time Katherine realised how very handsome he was. She pushed that thought firmly away; she had fallen for a handsome face but once in her life and it had been a salutary experience.

"I am not thrown as a matter of course, my hornet, but was referring to my time at Waterloo. It usually takes more than one shot to dismount me, but thankfully I am out of practice at dodging bullets."

"Then you should not allow your friends to shoot across the road," she said a little tartly; the handsome gentleman who had disappointed her had also been a soldier.

"My friends?" Harry queried.

"Could you take off your cravat, sir? I need it to bind your wound. You are, I assume, Lord Treleven?"

Harry inclined his head.

"Well if the shot wasn't caused by one of your friends shooting pheasants, how do you account for it?"

"Probably a poacher," Harry said, wincing as he lifted his arm to loosen his cravat.

"Here, let me," Katherine said briskly. "You are making the wound bleed even more."

She dealt with the neckcloth in a businesslike manner, keeping her eyes firmly fixed on the job in hand but not quite managing to avoid them slipping for the briefest moment, to observe the strong column of his throat as it was revealed.

"Very efficient," he murmured softly, causing her to glance up. His eyes had darkened to a disturbing sapphire blue. "Anyone would think you had done this before."

Katherine yanked the now undone cravat none too gently, causing her patient to wince as the friction caused a momentary flash of heat to sear his neck. "It is hardly a difficult task," she snapped. Retrieving her scissors she cut it neatly in two.

Harry groaned. "First my shirt, now my cravat, you are quite ruthless, Miss Lockhart, whatever will my valet say?"

"Are you never serious?" she chided as she folded one half of the cravat into a neat pad and pressed it quite firmly against the wound.

Harry sucked in a deep breath.

"I am sorry but it must be done if we are to stop the bleeding," she informed him, wrapping the rest of the neckcloth around his arm and tying it as tightly as she could.

"There," she said, finally satisfied. "That should do until the doctor is fetched."

The sound of hooves galloping towards them caught their attention.

"Ah, Kenver," Harry smiled, as he pulled up beside them. "I thought you might arrive before too long."

"An' well you might, sir, what with that showy new stallion of yours arriving in a lather as if all the hounds of hell were after him!"

"We must not blame Hermes, Kenver, someone has been shooting in the woods and he has not been trained to ignore gunfire, after all. I hope he has taken no hurt?"

"No, sir, he's just spooked is all, but seeing as you're one of the best horsemen I've ever seen, I couldn't account for it unless something serious had happened."

"It is nothing," Harry assured him. "I was caught napping, Kenver, wool-gathering, so my reactions weren't quite up to the mark. I do hope you did not mention your concerns to my mother?"

"Didn't have to, sir. She saw the horse come flying back alone and came immediately to alert me."

Harry frowned. "I am afraid I am going to have to relieve you of your mount, Kenver, but Miss Lockhart has been most eager to help, so I am sure she will not mind if you ride with her coachman on the roof of her carriage."

Katherine followed this exchange with some interest; she always felt you could tell a lot about a person by how they dealt with their servants. It had been immediately apparent that Kenver had been concerned for his master; his deep-set dark eyes had held a world of worry as he had galloped up and his brow had been deeply furrowed. It was still furrowed, as if he were not quite happy about Lord Treleven's explanation although he said nothing more.

"You cannot be foolish enough to ride when you have lost so much blood!" she protested. "I am quite prepared to take you up in the carriage, Lord Treleven."

Harry mounted the horse with ease and grinned down at her. "I am not such a poor creature. I will go ahead and warn my mother of your arrival, Miss Lockhart. Thank you for your kind ministrations, but I will do now."

With that he took off down the avenue at quite a pace, his blond locks flying and his white shirt ruffling across his broad back in the breeze.

"Of all the stubborn, foolhardy—" Katherine broke off as she remembered Kenver.

"He may be both of those, ma'am, but he could ride a horse in his sleep," he said, picking up the ruined coat that still lay in the dust. He observed the torn, bloodied sleeve for a moment and shook his head. "Barring unusual circumstances," he added under his breath.

What an extraordinary woman, Harry mused as he rode back to the house. There was nothing remarkable in her looks, apart from her hair, whose glossy brown sheen reminded him of a ripe conker, and perhaps her eyes. Yes, it was her eyes that gave her distinction, they were, he supposed, hazel but their predominant colour seemed to alter with her mood. At first they had reminded him of clear warm honey but when they had flashed at him, the bright emerald flecks that had darted across them had made them appear more green than gold.

He gave a dry laugh. Distinctive they might have been, but he was not at all sure he approved of the possessor of them. He liked his women feminine and skilled in the art of flirtation and Miss Lockhart was anything but; her pelisse had been of a dull grey that had leached all the colour from her complexion and her bonnet had been practical but unadorned with any frivolous ribbons or flowers. Managing and eccentric were far more appropriate epithets for her.

He unconsciously rubbed the back of his still warm neck. Most of the respectable females of his acquaintance would have blushed adorably and fluttered their eyelashes at him if they had had the audacity to remove his cravat in the first place, something he took leave to doubt, but not Miss Prim and Proper; instead her eyes had flashed disdain as she had torn it from him. Any delicate female could also have been expected to at least feel queasy at the sight of his wound, but Miss Lockhart's warm smile after she had been allowed to inspect it had been of the sort he usually received after delivering a well-chosen compliment. He wondered from where she had sprung.

More pressing however was the question of the poacher in his home wood. He had made light of it, but either things had become very lax in his absence or the locals were getting desperate for food. Either way, it was an unwelcome development he would have to deal with. He would go and see Mr Caldwell tomorrow. He could not imagine why he would bring in his own workforce when there were plenty of willing and able men and women in the vicinity.

He found his mother pacing up and down in

the stable yard, wringing her hands. Almost as soon as he had dismounted she crossed quickly to him and clasped him to her as she choked back a sob.

"Come now, Mother," he soothed, returning her embrace and holding her to him for a moment. "There is no need for you to be so distressed, I met with a small accident but am not much hurt as you can see."

Putting her gently from him, he looked down into the blue eyes so like his own, which were at that moment brilliant with unshed tears.

"No need to feel distressed?" she gasped. "The last time a horse came home alone your father had been thrown and broken his neck!"

Taking her arm he led her back towards the house. "I am sorry to have caused you such worry and reminded you of so sad a time," he said softly. "But fortunately you will have no time to dwell on what might have happened for you have a visitor coming up the drive even as we speak."

"Oh no," Lady Treleven said reflexively. "I shall be away from home for I cannot face anyone just at the moment, you cannot expect it of me."

As they entered the house, they found Glasson, their butler, waiting for them.

"I am glad to see you safe, Lord Treleven," he said calmly, his impassive glance resting briefly upon Harry's arm. "I have already sent footman James to fetch Doctor Fisher in case he is required."

"It was quite unnecessary," Harry said, a trifle shortly.

"Thank you, Glasson." Lady Treleven managed a small smile. "Let me know as soon as he arrives. We are about to receive another visitor, you will tell them—"

"That Lady Treleven will receive them," interrupted her son, leading her firmly into the morning room.

"Really, Harry!" she protested. But once he had explained the circumstances of his accident and Miss Lockhart's unusual reaction to them, she changed her mind.

"What a remarkable young lady," she murmured. "I will of course receive her and thank her for her kind services to you, but I will have something to say to Mr Hewel presently, some measures will have to be put in place to keep future poachers out."

"You can safely leave all that to me, Mother," Harry said firmly. "Now, if I am not much mistaken your visitor has arrived and so I will leave you."

"No, Harry," Lady Treleven replied, just as firmly. "You will remain with me for the duration of her visit or until the doctor arrives, at least."

As Miss Lockhart was just then announced, he was left with very little choice, but relief that his mother had regained her usual equanimity overrode any slight irritation he might feel.

He turned and made his bow as she entered the room. "Please let me introduce you to my mother. Lady Treleven, Miss Lockhart."

Lady Treleven's face was wreathed in smiles as she came forwards and took Katherine's hand. "I am very pleased to make your acquaintance, Miss Lockhart, and must thank you for coming to Lord Treleven's rescue."

"No thanks are necessary," she smiled. "He would, after all, have been rescued anyway, only moments later."

"Nevertheless, your prompt actions were admirable and so very resourceful. Please sit down and tell me what I can do for you, for I am fairly certain we have not met. You are not, I suppose, related to Amelia Lockhart who was Amelia Grantley before she wed?"

Katherine's brows rose in surprise. "Indeed, ma'am, she was my mother."

"Oh, she has passed then? I am sorry, child.

I made my come out with your mother and we were friends for a few years, but we eventually lost touch when we married and moved to the country. My husband was not overly fond of town."

"Your brother wouldn't happen to be Richard Lockhart would he?" Harry asked.

"Why yes, are you a friend of his?" she asked, surprised.

"More acquaintances," acknowledged Harry. "I haven't seen him for many years but we were at school together." He looked a touch rueful. "If I remember correctly he was quiet and studious whereas I was always kicking up a lark so our paths did not cross very often."

"You surprise me, sir," Katherine said drily.

Lady Treleven hid a smile. "Your estate is near Bath is it not?"

"Yes, I have until recently been living with my brother at Felsham Court."

"You are a long way from home, Miss Lockhart."

They both listened with interest as she explained her present predicament. As she described the state of the house and gardens, Lady Treleven shuddered.

"It sounds quite uninhabitable, I am surprised you didn't turn around and head straight back home."

It was Katherine's turn to look a little rueful. "It was not an easy situation for either my new sister-in-law or myself," she admitted. "I have been used to managing everything, you see."

"You surprise, me," Harry murmured, throwing her own words back at her.

Ignoring him, Katherine addressed Lady Treleven.

"Apart from anything else, I think the property worth saving, only I need some advice on how to acquire so many persons almost immediately."

"Well, you could try Penzance, it is the largest town within easy reach," Lady Treleven suggested.

"No!" Harry interjected, rising to his feet. "Miss Lockhart, if you will be advised by me, I know where a number of local men and women who need work can be found instantly."

"Well, that's settled then," beamed Lady Treleven. "You may leave it all up to Harry, Miss Lockhart, one good turn deserves another, after all."

Harry noticed the slightly stubborn tilt to Katherine's chin and thought she would refuse his suggestion but after a moment's hesitation she nodded decisively.

"As long as they are hardworking and honest, I would be grateful for your assistance in this matter, Lord Treleven."

"And in the meantime, you and Mrs Abbott must come and stay with us. You cannot remain at Helagon until the work has been done, you will be most uncomfortable."

Katherine looked a little startled. "I would not impose on you so, Lady Treleven."

"Nonsense, child," her hostess said, getting to her feet. "It is the least I can do for the daughter of an old acquaintance and besides, you will be company for my daughter Henrietta, she is very shy and has few friends."

After a brief knock, Glasson entered the room. "Doctor Fisher has arrived, sir."

"I will take my leave," Katherine said rising to her feet.

"Not staying to observe the doctor's work, Miss Lockhart?" Harry quipped.

She smiled archly at him. "Not in this instance, Lord Treleven, your injury is not interesting enough to merit a second look."

Harry let out a bark of laughter and strode to the door. "On this point, at least, we are in agreement. I will come over in the morning with my steward, Mr Hewel, to cast an eye over what needs to be done, Miss Lockhart."

Lady Treleven walked her to her carriage. "I will expect you by tomorrow afternoon at the latest," she smiled. "And I will not take no for answer; if you do not arrive by then, I will come and fetch you myself."

CHAPTER 4

Doctor Fisher appeared to be a serious young man, the impression reinforced by the small-rimmed glasses that he wore. He confirmed Miss Lockhart's diagnosis and praised her prompt action and the neat job she had made of binding his wound.

"For as you have been a soldier, sir, I am sure you are well aware that it is infection rather than the wound itself that often leads to the loss of a limb or a life."

"You really must meet Miss Lockhart," Harry murmured. "You both have so much in common."

The doctor's lips quirked in amusement. It had not taken him very long to get Lord Treleven's measure. Apart from the fact that he oozed restlessness and barely restrained impatience, he had heard a few stories about him from Doctor Peasbody on his retirement.

"It is a shame things turned out as they did," he had said. "He was a great gun as a lad, always up for some fun and gig and inevitably getting into some scrape or other, whether it was tumbling out of a tree or falling into the river!"

After cleaning the wound and dressing it in a lighter bandage, he gave him a shrewd look.

"I don't suppose there is any use in my suggesting you take things easy for a day or two, Lord Treleven?"

"None at all," Harry confirmed cheerfully. "I have sustained far worse injuries and not been unduly incapacitated."

Doctor Fisher merely nodded. "Then I won't waste my breath, but if you do feel at all feverish or any extraordinary discomfort, please send word sooner than later," he advised. "You will find me at the parsonage in Langarne."

"I know. It is a strange place for a young doctor to try and make his name," Harry commented.

"Ah, but I don't wish to make a name, but rather learn my trade and offer help to those that need it. I am fortunate that my uncle has offered to shelter me."

Harry's lips twitched. "Tell me, how do you find Mrs Creedely?"

The doctor chuckled. "Caustic!" He picked up his bag. "If I don't hear from you in the meantime, I will be back in a couple days to change the dressing."

He found Lady Treleven hovering on the landing as he gently closed the door to Harry's chamber.

"It is really not too serious," he assured her, noting her anxious look. She was a handsome woman, but he did not miss the fine lines that remained etched on her brow even as she smiled.

"No, of course not," she said calmly enough. "But he was extremely ill with malaria until very recently and I fear is not yet quite as robust as he was. I tried to delay his return as long as I was able, for I knew he would have much to do when he came home." She paused, looking slightly melancholy for a moment. "I have not kept as close an eye on things as I should have in recent years, you see."

"My uncle informed me of your circumstances," Doctor Fisher said solemnly. "You have had much to bear, ma'am. Your concern is understandable but if I may offer a little advice?"

"Please do," she invited.

"I speak now as a son as well as a doctor, you understand. It has been my experience that one cannot force someone to go against his or her nature and expect a happy result. Even if you could persuade Lord Treleven to take things easy, his spirits would be sadly affected and that in turn, would impede his recovery."

Lady Treleven sighed. "You are right, of course. Indeed, you are wise beyond your years, Doctor Fisher."

"I do not know about that, Lady Treleven, but I have always enjoyed studying the human mind as well as the body. I truly believe the health of both is intrinsically linked."

They had been slowly making their way along the landing and had come to the top of the stairs. Lady Treleven impulsively laid her hand on his arm.

"I think you are a young man of sound sense, sir. If you wouldn't object to me trespassing on your time a little further, would you very much mind taking a quick look at my daughter, Henrietta?"

"Not at all, ma'am," he said promptly. "What is it that ails her?"

A small frown deepened the lines on her forehead. "It is hard to say," she admitted. "You will probably think me a complete worrywart but she did not come down today pleading a headache. It is probably nothing, she is very shy you understand and found her season very trying, although she perked up considerably after her brother returned. But since we have come home, she seems very lethargic again."

They found her sitting in the window seat, her long blonde hair unbound and falling in soft undulations to her waist. Her legs were drawn up and encircled by her arms and she was staring blindly out at the rolling landscape before her. She did not even seem aware that she had company until her mother spoke a little sharply.

"Henrietta, you have a visitor."

Her head snapped round, her eyes huge in her pale face.

"It is only Doctor Fisher come to see you," Lady Treleven soothed. "Harry met with a slight accident today—"

"Oh no!" she cried.

"There is no need to be alarmed, my dear, it is nothing too serious, but as the doctor is here, I thought we might just check that you are not sickening for something,"

"Oh, Mama, it is not necessary I assure you. It was just a headache and it has gone now," she said in a rush, colouring slightly.

"Well, nevertheless, you will let him examine you."

"Examine me?" she said alarmed, swinging her slippered feet to the floor.

Doctor Fisher had stood immobile in the doorway, but at her evident distress he moved a few steps into the room and bowed. "Miss Treleven, please do not worry. I will not do anything intrusive, I assure you." His cool, impersonal tone seemed to reassure her.

Henrietta gulped and turned back to Lady Treleven. "Mama, you will stay won't you?"

"Of course," she replied.

Smiling gently, Doctor Fisher approached her slowly as he might a frightened animal. "Now, Miss Treleven, I am simply going to take your wrist in my hand so I can take your pulse, it will not hurt I assure you."

Henrietta obediently held out her arm and watched in wide-eyed fascination as the doctor gently gripped her wrist and closed his eyes as if to concentrate.

"Well, all seems well there," he murmured after a moment.

He then seated himself on the window seat beside her and took her head between his hands. He immediately felt her stiffen and released her.

"Do not be alarmed, Miss Treleven, I just

wish to observe your eyes a little more closely and it helps if your head remains still. May I?"

Henrietta nodded and he repeated the gesture. "I am pleased to report, ma'am," he said gravely after a moment, "that they are not crossed at all."

Henrietta's face was transformed as she giggled.

Rising to his feet he smiled. "There, that was not so bad was it? I hope next time I see you, you will not look at me as if I am an ogre."

Henrietta blushed slightly but shook her head.

"I will just see the doctor out, my dear," Lady Treleven smiled. "Then perhaps you will take a turn about the gardens with me. Some fresh air will do us both good, I am sure."

"Of course, Mama."

"That was well done of you," Lady Treleven said as they descended the stairs. "It is not easy to draw Henrietta out."

Doctor Fisher looked thoughtful. "Physically there is very little wrong with your daughter, ma'am. But I think you are right, her spirits are low. It would have been useless to enquire into the cause of her melancholy on such slight acquaintance, but perhaps if she sees me when I come to call on Lord Treleven, she may eventually be persuaded to confide in me."

"Yes, you may be right. When next you come to call on my son, come in the afternoon and stay for dinner."

Harry was true to his word and called at Helagon the following morning. Miss Lockhart was busy writing a letter when he was shown into the library and looked up with a frown when he was announced. Clothed in a modest high-necked morning dress of jaconet muslin, her hair confined in a very severe style, she reminded him of a school ma'am who was planning her lessons and was not best pleased at being disturbed.

"Miss Lockhart," he said bowing. "I apologise if I have interrupted you but you were, I hope, expecting me?"

She stood immediately and smiled distractedly. "Of course, forgive me, it is not your arrival that has caused my consternation, Lord Treleven. I am writing, or rather, attempting to write to my brother about the sorry state of this property. He wishes me to put it in order but neither of us expected it to be quite such an undertaking."

Harry glanced at the abandoned letter on the desk. As he had expected, she formed her letters in a neat, legible style, but many of the uniform lines had been crossed and re-crossed, suggesting an indecision he did not immediately associate with her on his admittedly short acquaintance.

"It must indeed be a difficult task," he acknowledged, suddenly recalling that the nickname, Lockpurse, had been attributed to her brother for his penny-pinching ways. "If you paint things in too good a light he will not understand why you need to draw on his funds quite so frequently, but if you state the case too baldly, he may baulk at the expense and order you home immediately."

Katherine looked surprised at his astuteness. "You have it in a nutshell, sir," she sighed. "You make me sound like such a scheming creature, and perhaps you are right, but I had hoped to make my home here and the idea that I might be forced to leave so soon, is a lowering one."

"Come now, Miss Lockhart, all is not yet lost. Mr Hewel is already casting his eyes over the house and it may be that we discover the case is not so desperate as you suppose – and even if it is – console yourself with the thought that once it is brought up to scratch, your brother can make back his money any time he wishes to sell it. A mouldering ruin is certainly of no use to him."

Katherine's expression lightened. "How very right you are, Lord Treleven, in fact he would be making a good investment. That is exactly how I shall put it to him." She smiled gratefully. "Thank you, sir."

"Rescuing damsels in distress is my speciality," he grinned, offering her his arm. "Come, show me around this palace."

"I knew it wouldn't last," she murmured, sweeping past him, leaving him to follow in her wake.

"What wouldn't last?" he asked.

"You being serious for more than a moment. I suppose it was too much to ask for."

"Far too much," he acknowledged as he caught up with her in the hall. The stairs groaned their protest as he mounted them. "Well, you are at least in no danger from burglars, ma'am, they would not be able to come up these stairs without being heard for certain."

"Even if they did manage such a difficult feat, they would be poorly rewarded for their ingenuity," Katherine said drily, "for I cannot imagine what they would find that was worth stealing."

Harry could only agree as more of the house was revealed to him. But he suspected he had been in the right of it, it certainly looked bad on the surface, but he thought that once the roof had been fixed the rest wouldn't be too difficult to rectify.

They found Mr Hewel in the gardens with Mrs Abbott, deep in conversation. Once the introductions had been made, Katherine braced herself for bad news.

"It was very kind of you to come, Mr Hewel, but please put me out of my misery. How bad is it?"

"Oh, it is not as dire as you think, ma'am. You've caught it just in time. If it had been left for another year now, it would be a different matter. Once the slates have been replaced on the roof and the ceilings in the attic sorted, you'll be watertight. A few of the window frames and floorboards are rotten and will need replacing, but we have plenty of skilled men hereabouts – more than one of them has built his own house."

"Mr Hewel is also very knowledgeable about gardens, my dear," Mrs Abbott said. "He could see the potential of this one immediately."

Katherine smiled at her companion. "I am sure he could not fail to be infected with your enthusiasm."

"Indeed, ma'am," Mr Hewel agreed. "Mrs Abbott knows a thing or two about horticulture and has an eye for design."

"How long will it take to have the house habitable, do you think?" Katherine asked him.

"Well, barring complications, a few weeks should do the trick. I can have some men down here this afternoon if that suits, ma'am."

"Excellent. Perhaps I should delay my visit to Lady Treleven until I have given them their orders."

"That will be quite unnecessary, Miss Lock-hart," Harry assured her. "Unless you also have an unusual interest in repairing old buildings, I would leave Mr Hewel to oversee everything. He will appoint a trustworthy person to be in charge who will report to him."

For the second time Harry noticed the mulish set of her chin but her reason again over-came her desire to disagree with him.

"Of course. I freely admit that I would not know where to start, so I must thank you again, Mr Hewel, and can only hope the task will not be too burdensome for you."

The steward smiled. "I overlook repairs and

maintenance to our properties all the time, ma'am, it will be nothing out of the way, I assure you."

"Then I can only thank you. You will, I hope, keep me informed of all progress and costs involved?"

"As you wish, ma'am."

"Oh, and Mrs Nance will need a hand in the house, do you know of some girls who live locally who could help her out in the short term?"

"Leave it to me, ma'am."

"I will no doubt see you at dinner, Miss Lockhart, Mrs Abbott," Harry said, bowing and turning to leave with his steward.

"You may leave some of your usual duties to me whilst you oversee the repairs at Helagon, Mr Hewel," he said as they rode up the hill.

"That won't be necessary, sir," his steward assured him earnestly.

"I will enjoy it," Harry assured him. "You have so much to do already, it has occurred to me that as the estate is so large it might be a thought for you to engage an assistant to help you."

"You are not happy with my work, sir?" his steward replied a little stiffly.

Harry discerned the anxiety that lurked beneath his gruff words.

"You have held the estate together in my absence, Mr Hewel, and I am very grateful to you. You have not had an easy time of it either, what with the fluctuating price of crops and some hard winters and wet springs and I do not see things becoming any easier in the near future. We must also lessen the rents to make life easier for our tenants for they face the same problems, but we will need to think of ways to make up the shortfall."

He saw the older man's shoulders droop slightly. "Come, man, I do not wish to replace you and neither do I blame you for things you can have no control over. However, I am beginning to realise just how much you have to do on a daily basis. You can hardly have had time to look into things like better drainage and so on, but if you employed an assistant you would have time to investigate the latest developments."

They had reached the brow of the hill and came to a crossroads.

"You go on to Langarne, Mr Hewel, I am going to see our new neighbour. What can you tell me about him?"

"I have only ever seen him from afar, sir, but he is not liked hereabouts. He's thrown up some houses near his mine for those he has brought in and they keep to themselves mostly. You can imagine the bad feeling that exists amongst those who have lost their jobs. But it is more than that."

"Go on."

"There was a wreck about a month back, sir, and there were rumours, only rumours mind, that things were not as they should have been."

"How so?" Harry asked.

"Well, you know how it has always been hereabouts, if a ship flounders, those as makes it ashore are given shelter and food, but the local people harvest any goods washed up along the beach. They have always seen it as a gift from the heavens to help them through the hard times. They only heard of the wreck the next morning but when they went down to the beach, there was nothing to harvest apart from a few wooden spars and not a soul to rescue. They reckon Caldwell's miners had taken it all and some say that they may have caused it in the first place."

Harry looked startled. "That is a serious accusation. Is there any proof to back it up?"

Mr Hewel shook his head. "Not that I know of."

"Then I would ask you not to repeat those rumours to anyone else, Mr Hewel, it could lead to someone hanging by the neck."

"You're right, sir, and I haven't done so. It is probably just the rivalry between the newcomers and the locals that caused the talk."

Harry thought that Mr Hewel was probably right. The tales of wrecking were greatly exaggerated and he had certainly not heard of such a nefarious act on this coast in his lifetime. There were many fishermen in these parts and they would try and aid a boat in distress if at all possible, believing that to do otherwise would draw bad luck down upon them. But the country people would greatly resent anyone other than themselves harvesting the goods of a wreck; a right they had always seen as their own. They normally shared the goods between them, and his own father had usually found some offering left for him.

Harry was aware of a feeling of unease. For all the goods to have disappeared by morning, if indeed there had been anything washed ashore, there would have to have been an organised, co-ordinated effort to remove them. If there was another wreck any time soon, it could lead to a nasty confrontation between the country people and the interlopers. And whether it was intentional or not, Mr Caldwell was at the root of much of this discord.

As he turned into the gates of Thornbury

House, the words of the old man in Langarne came back to him, *'Things go to ruin when those as knows the land and its people leave it be.'*

He was only just beginning to comprehend the murky depths beneath those words. It seemed he had come home not a moment too soon. One thing was becoming clearer to him, however, he could not burst upon his neighbour and start demanding explanations for his actions, not until he was sure of the lie of the land, at least. If he put his back up at their first meeting, he was unlikely to find out anything of use or be able to persuade him that it would be better to employ the native inhabitants hereabouts rather than bring in foreigners.

Thornbury House had not been the principal seat of Lord Trewith and the estate was much smaller than his own. It was a fine house however, built in the Palladian style, boasting an impressive portico and possessing a pleasing symmetry. It was some years since he had been within its portals and Mr Caldwell had certainly put his mark upon it. He seemed to remember that it had felt like a country home should, with comfortable furnishings and old portraits lining the walls. Now it was decorated in a lavish, opulent style, and anything that could be gilded, was, particularly the elaborate frames of the many pictures depicting images of ships and landscapes from the grand tour. Modern marble statues and busts based on ancient Greek design lined the hallway and the ceilings had been decorated with spectacular plasterwork surrounding mythological scenes, some of which bordered on the indecent.

It seemed that Mr Caldwell was a very wealthy man and was not at all shy of displaying it. But the most exotic and startling item of all was his butler, if he could be called that. The man who relieved Harry of his hat and coat was of Indian descent. He wore a rich red satin turban and a matching garment that fell to below his knees, tied at the hips with a white sash. Trousers that clung very cosily to the leg, peeped beneath the hem.

He was shown into the library, a huge room that was filled floor to ceiling with gleaming leather-tooled books, their sheen undisturbed by so much as a speck of dust. He wondered idly if Caldwell had read any of them. Chairs and sofas were scattered about the room, all of them elegant with delicately carved legs, but not a one of them promising any degree of comfort.

The only slightly ungainly item was a large desk set in front of doors that led onto the garden. The long ruby curtains were half drawn to block out the sunshine whilst Mr Caldwell pored over a huge ledger. He unhurriedly marked his place, closed the heavy tome and rose to his feet as Harry approached.

"Lord Treleven, welcome, welcome."

The two men exchanged bows.

"Please be seated," he invited, nodding to the upright chair that faced the desk. "I must apologise for not having called upon you since your return, but I thought you would be inundated with old friends, at first."

"I appreciate your consideration, Mr Caldwell," Harry replied, noting that despite his jovial tone, his host's eyes were regarding him closely. He was, he judged in his late forties, his red face and rounded stomach suggesting he enjoyed an ample diet and a fine wine. Even as the thought flicked across his mind, Mr Caldwell reached for a fine cut glass decanter half filled with a rich red liquid.

"Claret?" he asked.

"I thank you, no," Harry smiled. "It is a little early for me and I have much to do today."

"I imagine you must," his host said, pouring out a generous glass. "It is never a good idea to take your hand off the tiller for too long."

"So I am discovering," Harry replied ruefully. "I have a lot to learn."

"Well, that is refreshing. I am afraid I have often witnessed young men who come into their inheritance arrogant and ignorant. Too determined to cling to the family traditions rather than branch out and ensure the continued fortunes of their families. But the world is always changing, young man, always changing, and if you don't move with it, I am afraid you will be left behind."

"I notice you used a nautical term, are you interested in ships?" Harry enquired politely.

Mr Caldwell chuckled. "I ought to be, I made my fortune through them, bringing goods back from India mostly, but it's a risky business and not as profitable as it once was. Besides, I'm not getting any younger and I've a fancy to settle down. When this place became available so close to the sea and with a mine attached, I snapped it up. I've never been one to let a profitable opportunity slip past me, you've got to keep your eye on the main chance, my boy."

Harry tactfully ignored such a term of address from one who was his social inferior. "I am beginning to think you are right, sir," he replied respectfully, "farming does not turn a profit as it once did. You must be doing something right for this house is quite splendid."

He had achieved his aim; the rather sharp

narrow-set eyes of his host seemed to relax, as did the man himself. He leant back in his chair and steepled his chubby fingers, looking thoughtful.

"I do not think your reputation does you justice, sir," he finally said.

Harry was all wide-eyed innocence. "My reputation, sir?"

Mr Caldwell chuckled. "Well, you were very young when you fell into folly and I am sure it was the lady's fault, but I had not expected you to be such a serious, respectful young man."

Harry dropped his eyes as if in embarrassment. "A few hard years having to earn my own crust has changed me, I think."

Mr Caldwell poured him a glass of wine, despite his protests.

"Nonsense, my boy, nonsense. We have a lot to discuss."

CHAPTER 5

By the time Katherine had conferred closely with Mrs Nance about her most pressing needs and all of her and Mrs Abbott's things were packed again, it was late afternoon and Helagon was a noisy hive of activity. Mrs Nance was in her element, issuing orders to the girls Mr Hewel had duly procured and shouting at the men who traipsed into the house to inspect the most damaged rooms, to take off their boots before they stepped foot on the newly scrubbed floors.

They arrived at Elmdon Hall to find Lady Treleven on the point of changing for dinner and were bustled upstairs almost immediately. She was shown to a lovely bright room with views over the rolling parkland in front of the house.

As Ayles unpacked her trunk, Katherine sat in front of her mirror brushing out her long silken tresses, a soothing pleasure she always reserved for herself. She was aware of feeling both pleasure and relief to be in such welcoming surroundings. Although an old house, Elmdon had been properly maintained and the furnishings were tasteful and comfortable without being at all ostentatious. She was, she acknowledged wryly, used to a certain level of comfort, and although she had been quite prepared to remain at Helagon during the renovations, she was glad for all concerned that this had not proved necessary.

Her family had never been fabulously wealthy but had always been able to command some of the elegancies of life. Their lands, whilst not overly extensive, were rich and fertile, bringing in healthy rents both from tenant farmers and a few modest properties they owned in Bath itself. Never having any inclination towards extravagance, they had always managed to live within their means and Katherine had learned well the arts of household economy from her mother.

She had always imagined that in the course

of time she would meet some suitable gentleman whom she would wish to marry and impress with these much to be desired skills. She had had no firm picture in mind of what he would be like, only that he must be sensible and of a steady character. She had no illusions of attracting anyone of great wealth or good looks as she knew she was nothing out of the ordinary herself and had only a respectable dowry.

She had hoped that she would meet this rather nebulous ideal during her season in London, something she knew her mother had been setting aside money for every year since she had been born. But this much anticipated event had never materialised as both her parents had met with an unfortunate accident when she had barely attained her seventeenth birthday. None of their careful planning and sensible ways had been a match for cruel fate. On returning in her father's curricle from a dinner with friends to celebrate the victory at Waterloo, they had turned a bend in the road and crashed straight into a carriage that had lost its wheel only moments before.

Katherine had been fond of her parents and had felt their loss keenly. Her studious brother had retreated to his study and she had taken up the reins of the household. Her season had not been thought of again and they had gradually settled into a comfortable routine.

Bath had no longer been a resort of great fashion, but when Queen Charlotte graced the town with her presence in 1817 on the advice of her physicians, there had been much excitement. She had shown her approval of Lady Isabella King's latest scheme – The Ladies' Association – a charitable organisation whose aim was to offer a home at Bailbrook Lodge to single ladies of gentle birth but little fortune. Katherine, approving of an institution that might relieve the uncertainty and situation of members of her own sex, had subscribed in a small way herself to the cause, and she had been persuaded to attend some of the celebrations held in honour of Her Majesty.

She had met the Honourable Mr Sharpe at one of these gatherings. He served with the 15th Light Dragoons who had come to the town as part of Queen Charlotte's escort. He had been very dashing in his uniform and had always had a smile on his lips. He had shown great interest in the scheme for the relief of impoverished ladies and had singled her out at every gathering she had attended, to such an extent that her friends had begun to tease her about when he would formally declare his interest.

When Princess Charlotte had sadly died in childbirth, the queen had rushed back to London taking her dragoons with her. Soon afterwards, Katherine had received a letter from Mr Sharpe. She had held it for a few moments before opening it, savouring the anticipation, her hand a little unsteady and a tremulous smile on her lips. At first, she could not quite comprehend the words that danced before her eyes, and had had to start again from the beginning, her hand trembling more violently as comprehension slowly dawned. Each and every word was burned into her memory, as was the humiliation she had felt.

Dear Miss Lockhart,

I am finding this letter a little harder to write than I had anticipated. I had not expected to genuinely enjoy your company, it almost made me wish to call a halt to the charade I was enacting. On reflection however, the discovery that you were a kind-hearted girl with an intelligent mind only further strengthened my resolve to bring you to a sense of your own folly.

You have fallen under the spell of the charismatic and influential Lady Isabella King and I am afraid are being led down a path that will not result in happiness for you or the females *The Ladies' Association wishes to provide for.*

Bailbrook Lodge will be a community of women – no more than a nunnery – but without the solemn vows that would bring the peace of an acknowledged vocation to God, or the security that such a calling might be expected to provide. Instead you will have an odd assortment of single ladies with no common cause to bind them apart from their indigence and desire to avoid the natural order that our society provides.

Some of these ladies, in their misguided quest for independence, will forgo and indeed reject the mantle of protection that their families can and should provide, thereby acting in a selfish and wilful manner. Others who are not so fortunate as to possess such a family, but having all the qualifications of a gentlewoman, and thus the means to provide for themselves through imparting their skills and knowledge to others – thereby becoming useful members of society – will instead band together like a disgruntled flock of crows. They will console each other over their perceived misfortunes until they can only be made happy by the misfortune of someone even more unfortunate or despondent than themselves.

The ideal of some sort of female utopia, in which females can live in harmony and somehow provide for themselves by pooling their limited resources is ridiculous in the extreme and can only end in failure.

My friends and I firmly believe this. We faced many

dangers and hardships when we fought, and eventually conquered, Napoleon. Many of our friends lost their lives in the endeavour, but we willingly sacrificed much in the name of King and country. We wished to ensure and uphold the values of our own nation, a nation led by men for the benefit of all.

Do not waste your time on such a cause as this, Miss Lockhart, for you do no good for society by doing so and although I admire your desire to help those you perceive as less fortunate than yourself, I would suggest you turn your eyes in the direction of those that truly need your philanthropy; the poor, the hungry, the sick – in other words – those who cannot help themselves. The poor woman starving in the gutter would happily give up her 'freedom' to be able to look after another if it provided a roof over her head and put food in her stomach.

I am fully aware that you are not indifferent to me, Miss Lockhart, and I sincerely hope that I have not touched your heart too deeply. It was not my intention to cause you lasting unhappiness, but merely to show you that it can be engaged, and will be again if you but let it.

There, my lecture is over. I hope you will not dismiss my words out of hand because I have hurt you or let this lesson turn you into the very thing I wish you to avoid becoming, but fear you may if you continue to keep company with such ladies; a bitter spinster. Do not worry that your name will be bandied about in relation to this matter, it was not done to cause you harm.

Although I doubt you will believe it, I wish you well.
Your friend,
Mr Sharpe

Hot tears had poured down her face on reading this missive, followed by a furious anger that she had been duped so. She had torn it into shreds and thrown it into the fire. She had never mentioned the letter to anyone and had laughed off any suggestions that she must be disappointed at losing her friend so soon, merely commenting that the light flirtation had been a pleasant distraction.

"Are you feeling quite the thing, ma'am?"

Ayles bustled into the room, her attitude as improved as her surroundings.

"Why, yes, of course," Katherine murmured.

"Only you looked as though you was carved from stone, ma'am, so still and bleak looking as you were."

"I was just daydreaming, Ayles. You may put up my hair now."

"How would you like it tonight, miss?"

"I really do not mind, do as you please," she said quietly.

A sudden gleam brightened her maid's eyes, although Katherine was too distracted to see it.

"That I will, ma'am, that I will."

All that abominable man had shown her was

how easy it was to be misled by the tenderer emotions of the feminine heart, how vulnerable they made one to manipulation, and how infatuation or love clouded sound judgement. She had certainly not made hers available for such abuse again.

With hindsight, she could not deny that he had been correct on some points. The charity had indeed faced some financial hardships and their continued security was uncertain; the ladies had been forced to move to a house in Bristol when the owner of Bailbrook Lodge had decided to sell the property. Katherine had turned her attentions to the infirmary in Bath and so had ended up following some of Mr Sharpe's advice after all.

How he would laugh now when her own circumstances were as he described, she must live on her brother's charity, become her sister-in-law's slave, or turn her hand to some gainful employment.

She unconsciously let out a dry laugh causing Ayles to look at her in some concern. It had just occurred to her that the doubt Mr Sharpe had cast upon a group of women being able to live together in any degree of harmony now seemed quite prophetic when she had not even managed to rub along with Caroline. She was not, she accepted, of a meek disposition. It could hardly have been otherwise when she had taken on the running of a quite large household at such a tender age, and she would indeed find it difficult to bow to rules voted on by committee, whether it be made up of men or women.

That did not mean, of course, that she agreed with his wide sweeping generalisations on the selfishness of women living according to their own desires rather than within a patriarchal hierarchy that was hostile of any challenge to its authority, or that her admiration for Lady Isabella King had in any way diminished; the Ladies' Association had only been one of many charities she had supported.

She certainly did not think it inherently selfish for an impoverished but educated gentlewoman to wish to live outside of servitude, whether it was paid or not, and could only admire that a lady who was independently wealthy had spared the time to think of others less fortunate than herself. But she could now see that the world was not yet ready to accept the principle of a group of ladies living in a mutually exclusive beneficial environment as a general rule, and that it would not suit everyone, certainly not herself.

In setting Helagon in order, she was at least

being useful to her brother in some small way. But the sad truth remained, once the work was finished, she must either agree to be dependent on his support or insult and upset him by applying for a genteel position that she had no wish to fill.

"There, Miss Lockhart," Ayles said, in an unusually softened tone.

Katherine raised her eyes to the mirror in front of her and blinked. Usually in a hurry and completely disinterested in impressing any of the males of her acquaintance, she generally asked for a simple, almost severe style that suited her no-nonsense personality. But given the rare opportunity to display her own creativity, Ayles had created a gentler look.

Although her gleaming locks were pinned neatly, she had surrounded them with delicately woven plaits, and soft waving tendrils had been allowed to frame her face. The result was very feminine.

Katherine's eyes slowly rose to meet her maid's and a small smile curved her lips.

"It is very pleasing, Ayles. Thank you."

Her smile was tentatively returned. "You have such beautiful hair, ma'am, it is a shame not to show it to its best advantage."

She disappeared into the adjoining dressing

room, in a moment returning with a simple dress of gold silk, rather short in the waist and sleeves. Katherine eyed it warily. It had been an impulse purchase that she had made when besotted with Mr Sharpe and she was yet to wear it. It hung a little off the shoulder and was cut lower around the bosom than she was used to.

"Come now, miss, it is really very elegant. Try it. It won't take a minute to change if you don't like it, after all."

Not having the heart to snuff out Ayles' rare good humour, she allowed her to have her way.

"There," she said satisfied, a few moments later. "You do me proud, ma'am."

Katherine looked uncertainly into the mirror. "You do not think it a little immodest?"

Ayles sighed. "No, miss, it suits your slender figure to perfection and adds length to your neck."

Katherine suddenly smiled, for the first time beginning to fathom the real source of her maid's dissatisfaction. "Poor, Ayles, I must have been a sad trial to you with my sober tastes and lack of flair."

"I have flair enough for us both, miss, if you would but let me show it."

Katherine laughed. "Be happy that I have let

you show it tonight, Ayles. My wardrobe is not filled with dresses such as these."

The maid looked at her with an eager look in her eyes. "There's nothing wrong with your dresses, ma'am, that a needle and thread can't fix."

"Perhaps," acknowledged her mistress.

Katherine took another long look at herself in the glass as Ayles made to leave the room.

"Wait a moment," she said impulsively.

Ayles looked over her shoulder, her hand still on the door handle. When Katherine hesitated, she turned and waited patiently.

It had occurred to Katherine that only yesterday she had watched Kenver closely to see how loyal he was to his master, taking it as a measure of Lord Treleven himself if his servant showed concern. Yet she had not given her own maid much consideration at all. It was true that she had not been in her employ long, and that she had not seen much to impress her, but it now occurred to her that neither had she treated her with the kindness or the patience that perhaps she deserved.

"I think we may have got off on the wrong foot, Ayles. Not only have I not given you the scope to do the job you have trained for as you would wish, I may also have been a little prickly lately. I have had a lot on my mind."

Ayles nodded cautiously. "And so you have, ma'am. I was not best pleased to be leaving Bath I must admit, but things are not as bleak as they first appeared." She suddenly grinned. "And it might have been for the best after all, for if I had had to put up with that trumped-up maid of Lady Lockhart's looking down her long nose at me much longer, I might have been tempted to tweak it!"

"She was not welcoming?" Katherine asked, surprised.

Ayles gave a harsh laugh. "About as welcoming as an upset stomach! She loved to brag about how fine her mistress looked and she had the effrontery to call you dowdy, ma'am. Not in front of the other servants mind, steadfastly loyal to you they were, wouldn't have stood for a word being said against you."

Katherine looked thoughtful. "Well, Ayles, you may take your needle and thread and do as you please with it. I will not have you suffer such an insult again."

Ayles curtsied briefly. "Indeed I will, ma'am, and there's no time like the present."

"Don't get too carried aw—" she began, but the reformed maid had already bustled out of the room with an air of purpose and a spring in her step that her mistress had never before witnessed.

When she entered the drawing room she found a young lady idly tinkling the keys of a pianoforte that stood in one corner. Any fear that she may have been overdressed for a dinner in the country was instantly dispelled for the young lady was very smart. Her attire was of the latest fashion – a round dress of delicately striped net over a white satin slip with pretty puffed sleeves decorated with small pink bows – the motif repeated above the trim of four rouleaux of pink ducape. It was charming and suited her fair colouring admirably.

"Hello, you must be Miss Treleven for you bear a striking resemblance to your brother," Katherine said conversationally.

The young woman stood and smiled shyly. "Yes, everybody says so, but I am not very much like him in character, I am afraid."

Katherine quirked an enquiring brow. "Why be afraid? I am nothing like my brother either, nor should I wish to be. I am sure you have a perfectly fine character of your own, Miss Treleven!"

"It is kind of you to say so, Miss Lockhart,

but I am afraid I am a mouse and my brother a lion."

Katherine seemed to consider this seriously for a moment. "How splendid," she finally said. "I think lions are vastly overrated, don't you? It is easy to be brave when you are bigger and stronger than most of your prey but just consider for a moment, all the advantages of being a mouse."

Holding her hand up in front of her, she began to count them off on her long tapering fingers.

"One, they are curious quiet creatures and so may observe much to their advantage. Two, they are modest by nature and so must always please. And last but not least, they have very good hearing and so can easily avoid unwanted guests."

Henrietta's smile added a sparkle to her lacklustre eyes, transforming her appearance from insipid to quite beautiful.

"What is this about unwanted guests?" Harry strolled into the room with Mrs Abbott on his arm. "You cannot mean this lady," he said, bowing over her hand, "for she is quite charming."

Mrs Abbott's face creased into a smile. "I

think there are other ladies present who deserve your compliments more than I, Lord Treleven."

She looked at Katherine and Henrietta and sighed approvingly. "You both look beautiful, my dears."

"Please, come and sit down," Henrietta invited, taking her arm and leading her to a comfortable looking sofa by the fireplace.

Harry turned to Katherine, his eyes slowly drinking in her appearance. Katherine might have bristled at his leisurely appraisal if she had not been similarly occupied herself. He was dressed as exquisitely as his sister; his coat of dark blue superfine clung to his athletic figure and his neckcloth boasted a sapphire tiepin and an impossibly complicated knot.

"I am glad it was not tied so when we first met," Katherine said softly, almost to herself. "For I would never have undone it."

The blue eyes before her held a twinkle as their owner took her hand and murmured, "You are indeed…the prettiest Kate in Christendom."

It appeared for a moment that he might drop a kiss upon the hand he still held. Katherine withdrew it hastily for his words stung even as her fingers tingled. She recognised the play from which he had stolen the words –

Shakespeare's *Taming of the Shrew*. Tilting her chin, she replied in kind.

"I see a woman may be made a fool, if she had not a spirit to resist."

Harry threw back his head and laughed. "I see I must pick my words and plays more carefully, Miss Lockhart. Forgive me, I meant no offense."

"Of course, Lord Treleven," she replied stiffly, inclining her head graciously. "How is your arm?"

"There is no use expecting an honest answer, my dear," Lady Treleven said, coming just then into the room. "I do not pretend to understand why men must think it a show of weakness to admit to pain, but so it is. Doctor Fisher will be here tomorrow to ensure all is well, however. He is a very sensible young man, I warmed to him immediately and have invited him to stay to dine."

"Then we will be a small party, Mother, for I have also invited Mr Caldwell."

Lady Treleven looked surprised. "Oh, I see. Well, I suppose one must get to know ones neighbours, after all."

"Is there any reason you would not wish to receive him, ma'am?" Harry asked, picking up her doubtful tone.

"No, dear, we have never had much to do with him. He did not take up residence until just before we left for town, for he set an army of men from London to alter the house to his own personal taste before taking possession of it, although it was a perfectly presentable house when he purchased it."

"You would not recognise it, Mother. Mr Caldwell has everything of the finest."

"Indeed?" his mother said coolly. "Well, it does not surprise me. He did call on us once or twice before we left and was very affable, if a little overwhelming and a trifle vulgar." She turned to Katherine and smiled. "Perhaps it is for the best, my dear, for he is your neighbour too and you will be more comfortable meeting him in company. In fact it could not be better, for we will be a larger party than you suppose, Harry."

Katherine noted that Henrietta had begun to look a little anxious.

"I think you will be pleased, Henrietta, when you discover who it is," her mother reassured her. "I thought you and Lady Hayward had become firm friends whilst we were at Eastleigh?"

"Oh, yes, Mama," she smiled. "But I am surprised we are to see her so soon or that Lord

Hayward will let her travel so far in her condition."

Lady Treleven laughed. "Oh, she is hardly showing yet and anyway, what Belle wants, Belle gets. But in this case he is the reason for the visit, my dear. It was unfortunate that some business or other prevented him joining us during our stay with Sir Philip, but it appears that he spent some happy times in this part of the country when he was a child and now that he has an expanding family of his own, is thinking of acquiring a property in Cornwall. In fact, they are bringing little Edmund with them, for Belle says that he has completely recovered from the measles and she cannot bear to be parted from him a moment longer."

"It seems you are to be inundated with guests, ma'am," Katherine smiled. "If the burden is too great we can easily remove either to Helagon or perhaps a hotel?"

"Nonsense, Miss Lockhart, it is far too long since this house was full of company. Oh, that puts me in mind of something, we will be an odd number for dinner. I shall also invite Mr Gulworthy. Doctor Fisher is his nephew, you know."

CHAPTER 6

After the ladies withdrew from the dining room, Harry retreated to his study to take his glass of port. Leaning back in his comfortable, leather, wingback chair, he stretched out his long limbs, crossed his ankles and sipped at the deep red liquid appreciatively. His father had always kept a fine cellar. He wondered how he would have dealt with Mr Caldwell. A sudden laugh shook him. He would have dampened his pretensions with a look. The old gentleman had been a high stickler. For a moment, Harry could almost feel his presence in the room and his voice sounded in his mind.

"Don't have anything to do with him, my boy, he's a vulgar, encroaching mushroom. Worships at the alter of Mammon, doesn't care for anybody but himself."

Harry sighed. He did not have the luxury of ignoring Mr Caldwell. He was fairly good at assessing his fellow man and had known he was not to be trusted the moment he had set eyes on him. Some instinct had warned him that he must play a deep game if he was to discover why he had really brought in his own men to the detriment of the country people. It had occurred to him that the cost of bringing them over and housing them must far outweigh any advantage that he might gain from them offering lower bids on their contracts. It also suggested he intended to keep them there for the foreseeable future.

He had not been best pleased to discover he was expecting houseguests and really did not have the time to entertain Hayward, someone he hardly knew. He could only hope that his hunt for a suitable property would keep him out from under his feet.

He was happy Henrietta would have the benefit of a friend, however, for he had been quite shocked at how timid she had become. She had only been a child when he had fled, and although quiet and sensitive, he could not recall her being as withdrawn as she was now.

He frowned and took another sip of his drink. He had a lot to answer for. His reckless behaviour had caused his family much anguish. It pained him that the last memories his father had of him were less than satisfactory. He had been so proud of him, at first, when he had returned from Waterloo and had not understood the gradual change in his son. Harry had hardly understood it himself. He had suffered a head injury and lost his memory of a significant part of the final day of the battle, but he had remembered feeling terrified and known that he had been found with one of his closest friends, Lieutenant William Hunt, dead atop of him. The nagging thought that he had done something cowardly had haunted him until he had all but convinced himself he had been trying to desert and William had died trying to stop him. Although he had told himself time and again that for him to act in such a way would be thoroughly out of character, he could neither bring himself to completely discount the theory or to share his fears with anyone. In the end he had attempted to drown them out with drink and wild living.

His mother's suffering at his antics and subsequent disappearance was carved into the lines that had etched themselves into her face. Poor Henrietta had lived in the long shadow cast by all the pain he had caused and it had all been so unnecessary as it turned out. The fever that had consumed him whilst he suffered with malaria had cast him into a nightmarish hell where he had relived every moment of that elusive day until he had finally remembered what had happened. He had not been cowardly at all, but had been trying to save his friend when a bullet had whistled past him, slicing the side of his head and sending him into oblivion.

Draining his glass, he reflected that he could not change the past, only shape the future. He was determined that Elmdon would become a place where they could all find peace and happiness again. Perhaps it was fortunate after all that they were to have visitors, for Lady Isabella Hayward was charming and had an infectious sense of fun, she could be relied upon to enliven even the dullest of parties.

He had been delighted when he had walked into the drawing room to see his sister's face lit by a smile. His surprise that Miss Lockhart could make Henrietta laugh was only matched by the amazement he had felt at her altered appearance. It never ceased to amaze him how a change of hairstyle and apparel could transform a lady. The gold gown had suited her admirably, not only revealing a very slender figure that was rounded in all the right places, but an expanse of skin he would lay odds was as silky as the garment itself.

She had also been smiling when he entered the room and had looked warm and vibrant, it was a shame she had retreated behind the hauteur she donned like armour whenever she was made uncomfortable. That was his fault of course. For some reason he could not resist the compulsion to tease her. If he was completely honest, he had even for a moment wondered what it would be like to kiss those wide, plump lips. He gave a dry chuckle. Her gaze would probably have turned as deadly as Medusa's and transmuted him to stone in an instant.

The following morning, Harry went out very early and made his way along the coast to Trenance, a small fishing hamlet that nestled between towering cliffs. As he had hoped, he found Joseph Craddock sat on a small upturned barrel by his boat on the narrow strip of beach, mending his nets.

He stood quietly behind him for a few moments, watching his nimble fingers deftly weave in and out of the fine mesh and then sat down beside him on the gritty sand. Joseph gave no sign he had noticed his presence but unhurriedly finished his task and then glanced at the long legs stretched out beside him.

"You've scratched those fine boots of yours, Lord Treleven," he finally said, turning his head slightly and giving him a sideways glance. "It's a shame after all the time your poor man must have spent polishing them until they be as good as a mirror."

He could not have been much more than forty and his tightly curling black hair was still unmarked by grey, but his tanned face was mapped with fine lines and broken veins from years of exposure to the wind and weather. His eyes were as deep blue as the seas he fished and of an unusual intensity. They were regarding him closely now.

"Did you get a good haul, Joseph?"

"Not bad, the pilchards are runnin'. You ought to come out one of these nights," he said with the ghost of a smile. "It always used to blow your troubles away."

Harry gave a wistful smile. "I'd love to but it's not fish I'm after today, Joseph, but information."

The small wiry man got to his feet and began stowing his net. "I'm listening."

"I hear there was a wreck not so long ago but there was nothing washed up on the shore."

"They still grumbling about the ghost ship, then?"

Harry nodded. "Were you out that night?"

Joseph shook his head. "No, 'twere blowing something fierce, only a fool would have gone out. Word got round the next day and me and some of the lads went to take a look, see if anything could be salvaged, but by then the ship had broken up on the rocks. We had the customs men prowling about soon after, asking questions that no one had the answers to. Apparently, it was taking on water out at sea and the passengers and most of the crew were picked up by another ship in their convoy, but a skeleton crew stayed on board, sure they could make Padstow. Seems they were mistaken, but neither them nor the goods has washed up anywhere that I know of. Probably at the bottom of the briny."

Harry looked thoughtful. "Some are saying Caldwell's men harvested it before anyone else got a look-in."

Joseph shook his head. "They would. Working underground too long has addled their brains. Who would have been out to see it? Caldwell's miners live over the headland and those sorry little cottages he has built 'em are set on the far side of the mine. And before you spout any nonsense to me about fire-setting to lure them in, there was no sign of any fires and how would they have known that the ship would have sprung a leak and be headed for land anyways?"

Harry couldn't argue with his reasoning. Indeed he had not said anything Harry had not already told himself.

"Why are you so interested, anyways?"

"I don't like the bad feeling that's brewing, Joseph. More than one good man has turned bad when he finds himself down on his luck."

"Well there's only one person round here who might wield some influence over Mr Caldwell, and that's you, sir."

"I'm working on it, Joseph," he assured him. His countenance lightened with a grin. "I'll come fishing one of these nights, it will be like old times."

His eyes looked out across the deceptively calm water in front of him. Further out to sea he could see a dark heavy curtain of rain and knew that before long the water would have quite a different character as the wind beneath the approaching clouds whipped it up into a seething frenzy.

"Weather's changing, I'd best be getting back, Joseph."

The small, wiry man nodded. "Aye, but you've got a few moments yet. Before you go, sir, there's something I'd like to show you."

Harry followed him up the beach until it met the cliff. Here, a small recess in the rock housed a boat covered in a tarpaulin. Together they untied it and flipped it back to reveal a small boat in perfect condition.

"Betsy," Harry murmured softly, running a loving hand along the smooth wood. "You kept her for me."

Joseph's weather-beaten face broke into a broad grin. "I knew you'd be back some day, sir. You've got more lives than a cat and have always been able to look after yerself. I remember when I was first teaching you to sail, you'd had maybe two lessons but arrogant young cockerel that you were, you took her out on your own rather than wait for me to get back from the fish market. My heart was in my mouth when I sailed around the headland to find Betsy drifting and no sign of you to be had. How I would have explained it to your father when he had forbidden you to take up such a dangerous hobby, I don't know. I was never more thankful than when you swam in with no more than a graze on your head where the block attached to the clew of the sail had bashed you."

Harry laughed. "Knocked me clean over-board and the current swept me away from her. By the time I'd swum out of it the cold had sapped my energy and I only just made it to the rocks. I had to scramble around them until I could make the short swim back to the beach. I remember you tore a strip off me. It's the only time I've ever seen you angry."

"Aye, well you deserved it. Anyhow, I thought you'd be wanting her when you came home so I've kept her here, and made sure she's all's spic and span."

Harry shook his hand warmly. "You're a good friend, Joseph. I am most indebted to you."

"Ah, get away with you, sir. We know how to look after our own hereabouts."

After breakfast, Henrietta offered to show Katherine and Mrs Abbott the knot garden. Small hedges wove an intricate pattern with gravelled paths winding between them. Fragrant scents drifted on the breeze as small beds filled with marjoram, thyme, lemon balm, hyssop, rosemary and lavender filled the delicate gaps between them.

"This is quite beautiful," exclaimed Mrs Abbott. "I do so enjoy it when design and practicality go hand in hand."

Henrietta smiled at the older lady. "It is one of my favourite places to walk and think."

"I should think it is," she replied. "Such a soothing, sweet-smelling garden must be the perfect place for contemplation."

"And what is it you contemplate?" asked Katherine, privately finding the dainty walkways rather confining. She would rather take an invigorating walk through the parkland if she wished to chew something over.

"Oh, nothing really," Henrietta replied, colouring.

"Come, child," said Mrs Abbott gently, taking her arm. "Although we are only recently acquainted, you will find a sympathetic ear in both Miss Lockhart and myself."

"Oh, I know, you are both so kind," Henrietta acknowledged. "It is nothing really. You will say I dwell upon things too much and it is of no consequence, I am sure."

"Well, let us put it to the test," encouraged Katherine. "If you lock your troubles away they

will worry at you until they make you ill or overcome you at the most inconvenient of times."

An image of her brother's face, shocked and
immobile, as she had suddenly burst into tears at
the dinner table floated into her mind. He had
only asked her gently if she thought it had really
been necessary to purchase quite such an expensive fabric for the new curtains in the drawing
room.

"There's no need to take on so," he had said
when he had finally found his voice. "I am sure
you know best, after all. Whatever has come
over you, Katherine?"

Pleading a headache, she had fled upstairs mortified by her loss of composure.
She could never have confided in him – although they had a comfortable fondness for
each other, they were not close above the ordinary, and emotional scenes were anathema
to him.

"I did not enjoy my season," Henrietta
began quietly. "I really did not wish to go, but
Mama insisted that we must, for if Harry was
away much longer he might be declared dead
and then Elmdon would pass to some distant
cousin."

"Where did he go?" asked Mrs Abbott.

Henrietta told them about her brother's

duel, how he had fled the country and of his recent joyous return.

"Oh, how much your poor mother must have suffered," Mrs Abbott declared.

"Indeed she did," said Henrietta. "And then my father died soon afterwards. She shut herself up here and hardly ever ventured out for such a long time. So I agreed to go, to see if I could make her happy. I knew that if I found a husband it would be one less worry for her."

"But you did not find anyone who would suit?" Mrs Abbott encouraged her gently.

Henrietta shook her head. "I couldn't talk to all the fine London gentlemen. Not the way the other girls could."

"But surely all of that hardly matters now that your brother has returned?" Katherine said, putting aside the disgust she felt at his selfish and wanton behaviour.

Henrietta coloured. "No, no, of course not, I told you it was nothing."

But Katherine had not missed the flash of pain in her eyes and it struck a chord. "Are you sure you did not find anybody in whom you were interested?" she said gently.

Henrietta shook her head violently, but her eyes filled with tears that quickly overflowed and ran unchecked down her pale cheeks.

"Oh, my dear, whatever can have happened?" asked Mrs Abbott, rummaging in her reticule for a handkerchief and passing it to the afflicted girl.

It was some moments before she could contain her sobs, but slowly the tale came out in fits and starts. She had been at a ball when a Mr Carruthers had made her uncomfortable by being a little too free with his talk as they danced.

"T-told me I was a dashed fine filly and wouldn't he like to be the one who broke me in."

Mrs Abbott looked appalled. "Was he drunk? Or mad?" she exclaimed. "To talk to a young lady of refinement in such a way is despicable."

"Drunk, I think," Henrietta gulped. "For when he whispered it in my ear, his breath stank of strong drink."

"And what happened then?" asked Katherine softly.

"I wanted to run from the ballroom but knew I could not, it would cause such a scene and I would not cause Mama so much embarrassment. I tried to find her, but there was such a crush of people I couldn't immediately perceive her and I felt horribly faint. I went out onto the terrace for some cooler air; it was quite deserted and I tried to gather myself." Her shoulders started to shake and she returned the now sodden handkerchief to her face again.

"And did he follow you?" Katherine asked, beginning to guess the real cause of her distress.

Henrietta nodded, shuddering. "He pushed me against the wall and kissed me with his foul smelling mouth, and his hands pressed me where they should not have. I fainted."

Mrs Abbott's eyes had also filled with tears. "You poor child," she cooed, wrapping her arms around her. "It was quite abominable. What did your mother say?"

Henrietta took a step backwards and mopped up the remainder of her tears.

"Apparently she found Mr Carruthers standing over me looking quite put out. He told her I had felt faint and come outside for some air and, concerned, he had followed me. I came around a few moments later and Mama took me home."

"You didn't tell her?" gasped Mrs Abbott.

"No, at first I was too ashamed," Henrietta admitted. "And then Harry came home and I could not destroy her happiness. If he had dis-covered what had happened he might have called him out and had to flee the country again. I could not have such a thing on my conscience, neither of us could have borne it if we had lost him again."

"No, of course not," Mrs Abbott soothed.

"Come, let us walk some more," Katherine suggested. "You cannot return to the house until your eyes are less red."

Henrietta offered a weak smile. "I will show you the maze."

Katherine had expected to find a series of small hedges and was surprised to discover they towered above her in neatly clipped lines.

"Oh, but how wonderful," exclaimed Mrs Abbott, delighted. "But what a lot of work it must be to keep them so well maintained!"

"Yes," agreed Henrietta, "our head gardener, Phillips, takes great pride in them."

Katherine suddenly grinned. "I like a challenge and shall try and find my way to the middle, but you must promise to rescue me if I get hopelessly lost."

Henrietta had recovered her poise and her smile this time was genuine. "Of course, I will go first and make my way to the centre. If you get lost, I will call out to you so you will know my general direction."

"We shall split up, Mrs Abbott," Katherine said. "The last one to arrive must accept a forfeit from the victor, to be given at a time of their choosing."

Mrs Abbott's face creased into a mischievous smile. "I accept your challenge, my dear."

They disappeared into the maze in different directions. Katherine strode out purposefully, laughing as she came upon a dead end, time after time. Eventually growing frustrated, she had to call out to Henrietta before she finally found her way to the middle. There she found a fountain, and Mrs Abbott and Henrietta awaiting her arrival on one of the benches that surrounded it.

"Congratulations, Mrs Abbott," she smiled. "I am bested. What is to be my forfeit?"

"Ah, you stipulated it was to be at a time of my choosing, my dear, and I believe I will hold you to that. I will choose a forfeit at a time that I feel will benefit you."

"You begin to make me nervous," Katherine smiled.

Mrs Abbott gave a tinkle of laughter. "Oh, you may be sure whatever I choose, it will be done with your own best interests at heart, I assure you."

"Did you also require Miss Treleven's assistance to find your way?" she asked.

"No, she did not," Henrietta smiled.

The mischievous twinkle re-appeared in Mrs Abbott's eyes. "I have often studied maze design," she admitted. "They are frequently built on a variation of a theme, and after a few false starts, I managed to work out the pattern of this one."

"Oh, then you had a hidden advantage!" exclaimed Katherine. "That is hardly playing fair, ma'am."

Mrs Abbott chuckled. "You should never issue a challenge without first considering the experience of your opponent, my dear."

Katherine looked at her with new respect. "I see I may have underestimated you, Mrs Abbott."

Glancing up she noticed a dark band of cloud had covered the sky.

"We must go or we will be caught in the rain," she said.

As they emerged from the maze, the wind that the tall hedges had sheltered them from whipped their dresses around their legs and tugged at their bonnets.

Katherine took Henrietta's arm. "You really must not blame yourself for that shocking incident, Miss Treleven. I will not say that it was of no consequence, it was horrid and it is understandable that you should have felt quite overset by the whole experience. But I do think that you have dwelt upon it perhaps a little too much. Your reputation remains intact as does your honour, thank heavens. If you can overcome the melancholy this incident seems to have caused you, there is no need perhaps to inform your family of it, but if it continues to haunt you, you must, for they will be worried for you."

She felt Henrietta tremble a little. "No, I cannot, and you must promise me, both of you, that you will say nothing without my permission."

"Calmly now, my dear," said Mrs Abbott, taking her other arm. "We will not betray a confidence easily, but Miss Lockhart is right, you must not allow one unfortunate incident to colour your view of the world. For every cad out there, there are many more honourable gentleman, I am sure."

Henrietta nodded. "I am sure you are right but I fear they will never be acceptable to me, for every time a single gentleman comes too near to me now, I feel quite sick."

"Give it time," Katherine advised. "I was once made a fool of by a gentleman and at first it felt as if the world as I knew it was turned on its head, but the feeling passed, eventually."

Henrietta looked a little more hopeful. "I am

sorry you too had a bad experience, Miss Lock-hart, and if you have recovered from it perhaps I will too. I must admit that I feel a little better for sharing my experience with you both."

The first heavy drops of cold rain began to fall just as they reached the house. As they smiled at each other in relief at having missed the downpour, they heard a bright trill of laughter coming from the morning room.

"Oh, that is Lady Hayward," smiled Henri-etta hurrying forwards.

They found Lady Treleven and Lady Hay-ward seated together on a sofa, smiling indul-gently at a very young child with a riot of blond curls, who, happy to be released from the con-fines of the carriage that had so recently impris-oned him, was running in circles around the room. A very large gentleman stood by the fire-place, one arm resting on the mantel, his lazy eyes also following his progress.

As the ladies entered the boy came to an abrupt halt by a small table holding a rather fine cut glass vase boasting a colourful array of flow-ers. His large grey eyes regarded them seriously for a moment before he placed one chubby little hand on the table to steady himself, and stood on tiptoes in an effort to reach one of the blooms. The delicate table wobbled ominously, threatening to spill both the vase and its contents onto the floor. Before that seemingly inevitable event could occur, the gentleman moved with surprising swiftness for one so large, and scooped his son up with one long arm even as he steadied the table with the other.

He looked down at the small boy he had cradled in his arm as if he were no more than a small babe.

"Whilst I appreciate your desire to greet the ladies with a floral offering, Edmund, you really must try for a little more finesse," he drawled softly, gently placing him back on his feet.

"A bow is all that is necessary on this occasion," he said, proffering them one himself.

They smiled as the little boy obediently followed suit. All three ladies nodded their heads regally in acknowledgement.

Once the introductions had been made, Katherine smiled but excused herself.

"I hope you won't think me rude if I run upstairs to tidy myself up a trifle? The wind has, I am sure, given me a rather wild appearance."

"Not at all," Lady Treleven smiled, glancing at the rain that now rattled against the small panes of the large windows. "You go and change too, Henrietta, for I can see a few spots of rain have caught you, I am only glad you did not get quite drenched. I do hope your brother has found somewhere to shelter for he went out very early and has not yet returned."

Once Katherine had changed her slippers and allowed Ayles to tidy her hair, she slowly made her way along the upper gallery, looking at the portraits of the Treleven ancestors. She lingered for a few moments in front of one. A tall, rather raffish looking gentleman stood by a harbour, a huge ship anchored behind him. Although his hair was both darker and longer, something about his confident stance and the lurking twinkle in his eyes reminded her of the present viscount.

"I see you have found my notorious relative, Sir Marcus."

Katherine turned, startled, her eyes widening. Lord Treleven stood before her as if her thoughts had conjured him up out of thin air. His hair was plastered to his head and his coat and breeches were soaked through, moulding them to him like a second skin.

"Notorious? I was just thinking that I could see a family resemblance."

He raised an amused brow. "Are you suggesting that I too am notorious, Miss Lockhart?"

She had simply uttered the first thoughts that had come into her head, not meaning to link the ideas, and was about to refute the suggestion when Henrietta's words came back to her.

"Well, you have, I believe, fought a duel," she said, raising her chin a little.

She regretted the words almost as soon as she had uttered them. The laughter died from his eyes and she recalled belatedly that it was not her place as a lady and a guest in his house, to remind him of his past indiscretions.

"Oh, Lord Treleven, just look at you dripping all over my clean floor, go and get changed do, before you catch your death!"

They both turned to Mrs Bidulph. The small, slender lady stood looking sternly at him but Katherine thought she could detect concern in her dark eyes.

Harry glanced down in surprise at the little puddle that was collecting at his feet and offered the housekeeper a rueful smile.

"I am sorry, Mrs Bidulph, I had not noticed."

He offered Katherine a brief bow and strode off.

Katherine descended the stairs feeling a little mortified. She could not explain her lapse in good manners. Whatever his past had been, he and his mother had been more than kind in welcoming her into their home whilst the repairs to

Helagon were undertaken. And then there was the expeditious manner in which Lord Treleven had assembled a workforce, not to mention appointing his own steward to oversee the project.

If only she did not feel this absurd attraction to him; she did not trust or like it. She had not been surprised to discover his duel had been fought over a lady – flirtation seemed to come as naturally to him as breathing. It did not come naturally to her however, and made her uncomfortable. She paused at the bottom of the sweeping staircase as another unwelcome thought came to her. She had encouraged Miss Treleven in the belief that she had recovered from her own experience, hoping to offer her some comfort, but if she were so wary of being made a fool of again that she viewed any gentleman who paid her any attention with suspicion, then she really could not make such a claim. Was she turning into a bitter spinster, after all?

CHAPTER 7

D inner that evening was enlivened by the vivacious presence of Lady Hayward. She was a very beautiful lady with gleaming golden hair and sparkling grey eyes. Her delicate condition seemed to suit her, for her smooth fair skin had a soft sheen that seemed almost to make it glow. She exuded happiness and Katherine could not help but reflect that it was a shame the condition had not resulted in a similar happy state for her sister-in-law.

She was clearly well acquainted with the Trelevens and was not afraid to interrupt conversations or address anyone, regardless of their position at the table, but she did so with a charm that made it impossible to mind her complete disregard for etiquette.

A very real affection seemed to exist between herself and her lord. Katherine noticed that when Lady Hayward made an amusing comment, a small smile would curve his lips and his eyes would flick briefly in her direction. Whilst never neglecting either herself or Lady Treleven who were seated on either side of him, he was, it seemed, aware of her at all times.

"I noticed a gig I do not recognise in the stables, could it be yours, Miss Lockhart?"

Katherine turned her gaze in the direction of Lord Treleven. He was immaculately turned out as usual, and his black swallow-tailed coat only served to heighten the gleaming lustre of his blond locks.

"Oh, it has arrived then," she said, surprised. "I found it in the stables at Helagon but my coachman would not allow me to use it until he had looked it over. It seems it must have passed muster. I thought it would be useful to have a light vehicle I could use to visit Helagon and check on the progress there. I had not realised it would be ready so soon or I would have asked your permission first. I hope it is not inconvenient for me to keep it and my horse in your stables, Lord Treleven?"

"It is not inconvenient at all, Miss Lockhart, although I would have been happy to drive you over myself anytime you wished."

"That is very kind of you, sir, but I am sure you have better things to do. Besides, I prefer to drive myself."

"Are you sure that is wise, my dear?" said Lady Treleven. "It may be better to let Lord Treleven drive you, for the roads around here can be very narrow and winding, I am sure they are not what you are used to."

Katherine smiled at her hostess. "You need not worry, ma'am, I am believed to be a competent whip, I assure you."

"Splendid," chimed in Belle. "Then you may take me up with you. I have a desire to see this crumbling ruin, it sounds terribly romantic."

Katherine laughed. "Well, it is not quite a crumbling ruin, Lady Hayward, and I must admit, I did not find it at all romantic. What say you, Mrs Abbott?"

Mrs Abbott shuddered dramatically. "Oh no, I remember us arriving in the dead of night, the house only lit by the moon and not a sign of life until you rang that creaky old bell, and then that owl started hooting and the bats started flying."

Katherine blinked. She had not seen any bats.

Belle was entranced. "Oh, but how exciting. What happened next?"

"We had supper and went to bed," Katherine said drily.

"Yes, my dear," agreed Mrs Abbott. "But do not tell me you did not hear the trees tapping on the windows as if trying to gain entry, or that dreadful wind wailing around the corners of the house like a lost soul screeching its agony?"

"It sounds deliciously frightening," Belle smiled.

"I would lay odds Miss Lockhart was not at all afraid," said Lord Treleven, smiling slightly.

"You would win your bet, sir," Katherine replied. "I slept the whole night through and never heard a thing."

Glancing at the slightly disappointed look on the face of the lady opposite, she smiled. "However, my maid did not sleep a wink and also complained of mice running across her bed in the night."

Lord Hayward grinned lazily. "Now do not say you would have also have enjoyed that experience, my lady, for you dislike them above all things."

Belle gave a tinkle of laughter. "I know, it is quite ridiculous that such a small harmless creature can frighten one so much, isn't it?"

"I am not afraid of them, I once kept one as a pet," revealed Henrietta. "I kept it in a bird cage and fed it cheese. It really was very sweet."

Lady Treleven smiled. "Yes, one of the stable cats dropped it at your feet when you were just a girl and you scooped it up and insisted you keep it."

"What happened to it?" asked Mrs Abbott.

Henrietta shrugged. "It escaped. I found the door to the cage open and it had gone. Whether it managed to free itself or someone else released it, I do not know."

Katherine smiled across at her. "I would not be surprised if it had liberated itself, did I not tell you mice were observant creatures?"

Henrietta returned her smile. "I would also like to visit Helagon, I think."

"Then I will drive both you and Lady Hayward," said Harry. "For I believe Lord Hayward wishes to make some enquiries in Padstow tomorrow and you will certainly not both fit in Miss Lockhart's gig."

By morning the dark clouds had drifted away leaving a clear sky. A brisk breeze still blew but it was not enough to make riding in an open carriage uncomfortable. Ayles dressed Katherine in a close-fitting carriage dress of mulberry-coloured velvet with a matching high-crowned bonnet. She had added a trim of white fur around the base of the dress and at the end of each tight fitting sleeve, and a plume of white ostrich feathers on the right-hand side of the bonnet, which fell in a graceful arc to one side.

Katherine smiled at her maid. "Thank you, Ayles. I don't know how you do it but you seem to transform things from plain to elegant with just a few light touches."

Ayles smiled, pleased with the compliment. "It was nothing, Miss Lockhart. Your figure made the dress elegant as it was and I know you like things kept simple, but there's no harm in a bit of prettifying."

At the last moment, Lady Treleven and Mrs Abbott also decided to join the party and so she called for her barouche to be fetched to accommodate the small party of ladies.

Katherine, still determined to drive, went to the stable yard to collect the gig. She found both it and Lord Treleven waiting for her. He was dressed for riding and was tapping his riding crop against his thigh as if impatient to be away. It stilled when he saw Katherine and he offered her a small bow.

"As my services are no longer required and I have some business to attend to, I will only accompany you as far as the gates, Miss Lockhart. Unless of course, you would like me to cast my eye over the work being done at Helagon?"

"No, they cannot have got very far with the renovations after all, and I would not wish to keep you from your business," she assured him.

He stepped forward and offered his hand to help her into the waiting gig. She settled herself and took the reins in her hand before smiling her thanks.

"My stable lad, Jim, will accompany you in the seat behind," he informed her.

Katherine's brows arched upwards. "Thank you, sir, but I hardly think it necessary when Lady Treleven's party will also be with me."

"You will take him nonetheless," Harry said briskly. "If there were to be any sort of accident our coachman would be hard pressed to deal with both vehicles."

Katherine had not seen this side of Lord Treleven before and found herself bristling at his commanding tone, as well as his suggestion that there might be an accident.

Kenver walked Hermes into the yard and Harry mounted the chestnut stallion in one fluid motion. Katherine covertly admired his confident handling of the magnificent creature as he brought his skittish prancing under control with an iron fist on the reins. For the first time she caught a glimpse of the soldier he had been rather than the light-hearted flirt he had become.

Hermes was clearly longing for a good run but Lord Treleven kept pace with the gig as she tooled it down the long avenue, the barouche following sedately behind.

Katherine was aware that his eyes rested on her more than once, but she kept her gaze fixed firmly on the road ahead, not at all un-nerved by the scrutiny; she knew her own ability.

"You have light hands," he finally said ap-provingly.

A small smile of satisfaction curved her lips and she turned her head to observe him for a moment. "And you, sir, have a very fine seat."

Harry's eyebrows rose in surprise. "Was that a compliment, Miss Lockhart?"

"I am not such a hornet or shrew that I cannot give credit where it is merited," she said a little sharply, colouring slightly.

They had reached the gate and he doffed his hat to her. "Our ways part here. Be aware that the road down to Helagon may be slippery where the trees have prevented last night's downpour from drying."

Without waiting for a reply, he cantered off.

Katherine watched him for a few moments as she waited for the barouche to catch up. She was a little piqued that he had made no effort to apologise again for the shrew reference at least, but then he seemed unusually abrupt this morning as if his thoughts were elsewhere. She wondered idly what business could preoccupy him so.

Katherine had sent word of their visit ahead and they found Forster and Mrs Nance ready for them. The drawing room had been scrubbed and polished and it looked like they had scoured the house for the least faded chairs and sofas. They did not quite match and still looked a trifle shabby, but at least afforded a modicum of comfort to her visitors. The sun poured through the windows casting a cheerful light into the room.

"But this is quite civilised," said Belle, surprised.

"It is certainly much improved," smiled Katherine.

As she showed them around the house, they stumbled upon maids scrubbing and polishing in the bedrooms and workmen removing window frames or prising up rotten floorboards. The cracks and damp patches on the walls were still in evidence and where the ceilings were partially down in the attic rooms, buckets had been placed in various places to catch any leaks, some over half full of rainwater.

"Ah, now this is more hopeful," Lady Hayward declared. "If there are any spectres to be seen, it will be here that we shall find them."

Mrs Abbott looked much struck by this observation. "You are quite right, Lady Hayward, perhaps the wailing I heard was not the wind, after all."

Katherine smiled indulgently at her relative. Although she had called on her regularly at Felsham, her visits had often been brief and she had not suspected that beneath the gentle, meek appearance she presented to the world, lurked a mischievous humour. She rather enjoyed it and was thankful that her need for a companion had allowed her to get to know her more intimately.

The wind and rain of the previous day had prevented work on the roof, but a wooden scaffold tied together with rope had been constructed to allow access and a few men were removing the remnants of cracked and broken tiles.

The grass in the garden had been reduced to a much more respectable length and the paths were now accessible. The old beds had also been revealed and men worked to turn the long neglected soil.

Helagon was a hive of activity and Katherine received respectful nods or curtsies from the workers wherever they went.

"Lord Treleven chose well," she said to his mother when they finally returned to the carriages. "Everyone seems very respectful and hard working."

Lady Treleven smiled at her. "They are very grateful to you, Miss Lockhart. They have lost their work at the mine and have been having a hard time of it. This may only be a temporary reprieve for them, but it is a welcome one."

She thought over the words as she made her way up the steep hill that led from Helagon. It was, of course, Lord Treleven to whom they really owed their gratitude. She remembered that he had overridden his mother's suggestions about where to find workers with alacrity and determination. He had been very keen to help these men and women; he clearly took his position seriously, at least.

When they reached the gates of Elmdon, she realised she was reluctant to turn into them. She had never seen the sea and realised that she wished to very much. She drew alongside the barouche.

"Is it far to the coast, Lady Treleven?"

"Not at all, my dear, but perhaps it would be better if you wait for another day as Henrietta has promised to take Lady Hayward and Edmund into the maze and Mrs Abbott has offered to help me with some flower arrangements for tonight's dinner."

"Oh, I think I will just go and take a quick look if you don't object, ma'am. I have Jim with me after all."

"I can see you are determined upon it," Lady Treleven said. "And I must say you handle that gig very well, Miss Lockhart. As it really is only a very short distance, I can see no reason why you should not. Jim will show you the way."

They turned into a smaller track further down the road that led through the home wood. It was a pleasant drive; the trees were mature and there was enough space between them to allow the sun to create dappled pools of light. Katherine was enjoying listening to the birdsong when she thought she glimpsed movement amongst the undergrowth. Her shoulders tensed and her hands tightened on the reins as she remembered the poacher who had lurked in the woods on her first visit to Elmdon. A few moments later she saw a squirrel dart up the trunk of a tree. She let out a small laugh of relief but nevertheless flicked her whip to encourage the horse to go a little faster.

Presently they turned onto another track that soon led them out of the woods. They bowled along between fields, the grass was rougher here, and grey boulders were scattered across them reminding her of her journey across the moors. The breeze picked up as the prospect opened, and she saw a stretch of blue topped with white-capped waves. She turned onto the track that ran along the cliff edge and slowed the horse to a sedate walk. The furze and ferns gradually became less dominant and wild flowers wound their way through the long grass that waved in the fresh breeze.

She came to a halt and climbed down from the gig, wanting to get a better look at the coastline.

"Hold the horse will you, Jim?"

The skinny stable lad jumped down from his seat and obediently went to the horse's head.

Katherine walked towards the cliff allowing her fingertips to brush against the long grass. She stopped a few feet from the edge and gazed at the wild untamed beauty before her. She suddenly felt invigorated and wished for a moment that she could soar above the wide blue expanse like the white gulls that drifted gracefully on the breeze. Her eyes dropped to the golden sand that lay at the base of the cliff and she wondered how it would feel beneath her feet.

As her eyes wandered to the cliff face she saw the winding narrow path that led down to the beach below. Taking a cautious step forwards, she followed it until she could see that it could be accessed a few hundred yards ahead. She turned decisively back to the road and walked briskly towards the gig.

"I am going down to the beach, Jim," she informed the boy. "Walk the horse for me, please, I shouldn't be too long."

The boy looked surprised but knew better than to question his orders and so merely nodded.

The path curved its way down, winding back on itself several times, only now and then steep enough to require extra care. Katherine picked her way along it, thankful that she had worn her jean half boots, for the small stones that littered it would have made it most uncomfortable in anything less sturdy.

It was further than she had first thought and her legs were aching a little by the time she took her first step on the golden sand. She felt herself sink slightly into the soft, fine grains and made her way nearer to the waterline where it was slightly firmer, occasionally glancing back at the single track of footprints she had left behind her.

She walked to the end of the small beach where a tall black rock towered above her and skirting around it realised she could walk into the next, larger crescent-shaped cove. She amused herself picking up a few delicately shaped shells, pretty patterned stones, and fragments of smooth coloured glass.

Laughing as a sudden gust of wind tugged at her bonnet, she tied her ribbons a little tighter. Surprised at how far she had come, she realised she had lost track of time and reluctantly turned and began to make her way back, pausing when she saw something glinting brightly in the sunlight. Stooping she picked it up, placing it in her palm with her other treasures. She turned it this way and that – it looked for all the world like a diamond. She smiled to herself, it was highly unlikely of course, it was merely another fine piece of glass that had been shaped and polished by the shifting sands.

As she raised her gaze, a movement at the top of the cliff caught her eye. She saw a very small figure that must be Jim, waving frantically at her. She thought she heard a faint voice carried by the breeze and realised he must calling to her but she could not make out any words above the sound of the surf. It was she realised, noisier than before and her eyes turned back to the sea. Alarmed, she jumped quickly back as it nearly rushed over her boots. She had wandered up the beach in her search for shells and the sea had, it appeared, followed her.

She glanced down the beach and her heart began to hammer in her chest. Her footprints had disappeared and the water now engulfed the tall lump of rock that marked the cove she had found at the bottom of the path. She rushed forwards and stumbled, falling to her knees. Scrambling hastily to her feet, she picked up her skirts in one hand and began to run. Before she had covered half the distance she realised it was futile, her way was blocked and waves spumed white foam as they crashed up the rock face. Telling herself not to panic, she scanned the towering cliff systematically, searching for another way up. Her mouth dried as she realised there was none.

CHAPTER 8

Harry hastily untied the tarpaulin covering Betsy and pulled it back impatiently, laying it on the ground next to the small craft. He shrugged off his coat and laid it on top of the discarded cover. He was aware of a niggling feeling of guilt that he was going to indulge himself in a sail when he had assured Mr Hewel that he would ride out to see one of his tenant farmers. Mr Treen had sent a note to Mr Hewel asking to see him, but as he hadn't mentioned anything in particular, Harry didn't think it could be too urgent. He would go tomorrow; the weather on this part of the coast was often unpredictable and he might not see such perfect conditions again for weeks.

It wasn't the only thing that was unpredictable, he mused, as he pushed Betsy along the greased wooden planks Joseph had thoughtfully prepared for him. Miss Lockhart had looked very elegant this morning. The rich colour of her gown and the artfully placed feather on her cap had been very striking and although he had not been surprised to see she handled her gig with competence, he had not expected her to have such a confident, light touch. She could leave some of the incomparables who fancied themselves whips and liked to drive their phaetons around the park in town, in the shade.

Her compliment on his riding had taken him by surprise. There had been approval in her softened tone. Yet again, the urge to spar with her had overcome him and she had soon reverted to type. He should, of course, have assured her she was neither a hornet nor a shrew, but if he were to be back in time to greet his guests for dinner, he must hurry.

He pushed the small boat into the surf and jumped in. He reached for the oars and began to row, annoyed when he became aware of a slight twinge in his arm. When he was beyond the breaking waves, he set his jib and mainsail and Betsy immediately responded, skimming over the gentle swell. He raised a hand to a figure that had appeared on the beach. Joseph had come to watch him, but after a few moments he turned and made his way back up to his small cottage.

As the wind ruffled his shirt and hair, a wide grin spread over Harry's face and his eyes sparkled with pleasure. He had sailed in many ships, but for him, nothing could match the simple delight of a small vessel. Its performance and his safety relied solely on his wits and skill alone.

He raced around the headland and into the bay that marked his own land. It was then he saw the small figure jumping up and down, waving both his arms at the top of the cliff. He sailed in as close as he dared, knowing of the hidden teeth that lurked just below the surface, and realised the person was now pointing to the next bay.

Harry could sense the urgency in his movements and hurriedly tacked back out beyond reach of the rocks and then resumed his original course. The tall chimney of Wheal Trewith rose above the clifftop reminding him that he had not yet tackled Caldwell about re-employing at least some of his tenants at Langarne.

This bay, he knew, was not littered with the rocks that marked his own, and he steered a course towards the shore. The chimney disappeared as he came closer and his eyes fell to the beach below. It was then he saw the small figure in crimson, backed against the cliff face as the sea raced up the beach with the incoming tide.

Miss Lockhart! Wasting no time on pointless speculation as to how she had got herself into such a precarious predicament, he quickly furled his sails and reached again for his oars. When he was within striking distance of the small strip of beach that remained, he dropped his anchor over the side and slid into the water. He strode thigh deep through the swell, the incoming waves breaking around him and spraying his white shirt until it was also soaked through and clinging to him.

He was surprised that Miss Lockhart did not make any move towards him, but when he got close enough to see her eyes, he saw that they were large in her white face, and glazed with terror.

"Miss Lockhart," he said in the gentle tone he would use on a panicked horse, "you are safe now."

Her eyes fixed on his and the sound of his words seemed to slowly penetrate her senses. "You are real, then?" she whispered. "I have not conjured you up in my desperation to be rescued?"

"I assure you I am real." He smiled gently, stepping forwards and taking the hand nearest to him. It was cold and slightly damp from where it had been pressed against the slick cliff face. It curled tightly around his and he felt touched by her vulnerability. He quelled the urge to sweep her into his arms and reassure her further, sure she would resent him for it later and for once feeling no urge to tease her. Their eyes held for a long moment, the spell broken when something dripped on her face. They both automatically glanced upwards. Harry's brows drew together in a thoughtful frown as he realised they were stood beneath a dark opening in the rock.

"What is it?" Katherine suddenly asked, her voice a little stronger. "Is it a tunnel? I did wonder if I could escape that way only I could not find a way up there."

"It is a type of tunnel," Harry acknowledged, his urge to hurry tempered by his need to keep her calm. "It is called an adit, and its job is to allow the mine to drain so it does not flood. As it rained all yesterday afternoon and most of the night, I would expect it to be pouring with water today, spreading a red stain over the sea."

Imparting such a mundane snippet of information seemed to do the trick. She nodded her understanding and then glanced at the boat, which was swinging in the wind. Her gaze dropped to their still clasped hands and her brows rose as if in surprise. She quickly released his and took a small step away from the wall. A shaky smile curved her lips. "Whilst I am glad of your expertise in rescuing damsels in distress after all, sir, how is it to be achieved in the present case for I cannot swim?"

Aware that they had not long before the sea began to hurl itself against the unyielding cliffs, Harry scooped her up into his arms. "Like this."

He strode back into the water trying to protect her by turning his back on any waves that broke around them and hoisting her up as high as he could, but by the time he deposited her in Betsy, she was also rather damp.

He smiled as, regaining some of her usual dignity, she sat up ramrod straight, her clenched hands the only sign of her nervousness. He set his sails quickly before pulling up his anchor. A gust of wind immediately caught them and they shot forwards. Miss Lockhart looked startled and her hands opened as they sought to cling to the side of the boat. As they did so, the treasures she had collected went skittering across the wooden floor.

Harry let out a short laugh, aware of feeling

a strange mixture of amusement and annoyance.

"So, you risked your life for a few shells and pretty pieces of glass?"

Katherine coloured. "I was not aware I was risking my life, sir. I did not realise that the water would come in as it did."

"No, but what were you thinking, exploring without someone to guide you?"

"Lady Treleven saw no harm in it," Katherine defended herself, "and I had Jim with me."

"Neither of these arguments detracts from the fact that you put yourself in significant danger. I don't suppose my mother thought you would descend the cliff to the beach and as for Jim, it probably didn't occur to him that anyone might not know about tides."

She coloured and Harry realised he was being a trifle hard on her. Now that she was safe, all the ramifications of what could have happened to her had rushed upon him. If he had been many minutes later she would undoubtedly have drowned and he would not have been entirely without blame, for if he had accompanied her this morning as had been his initial intention, this would never have happened.

"Forgive me." He smiled ruefully. "It was not

your fault, just an unfortunate accident that does not bear dwelling on. Let us not quarrel but enjoy the sail back. There is nothing like it!"

The combined force of the wind and sun had largely dried them both by the time they reached the entrance of Trenance Bay, and Katherine had recovered from her ordeal enough to think that he might be right. Once she had become used to the strange movement of the boat and learned to move with it rather than brace herself against it, she had begun to enjoy the experience.

She watched, fascinated, as he constantly made small adjustments to the sails and the tiller and soon realised she was in safe hands. In truth, she had not doubted it from the moment he had taken her hand and she had realised he was flesh and blood, not a figment of her overwrought imagination.

Lord Treleven suddenly grinned at her. His eyes were glowing with pleasure and enjoyment. She found she could not look away.

"Give me your hand," he said softly.

It seemed to rise of its own volition. She looked on amazed as he stripped off her glove. He then placed her hand on the tiller where his own had rested only a moment before. It felt warm and smooth. As the small craft swung off course and the sails began to flap, he covered it with his own.

"Like this," he murmured, gently moving it this way and that. "You need to go where the wind can fill the sails. Close your eyes and feel it brush against your skin."

The moment she closed her eyes, she felt her senses heighten. The breeze whispered against her cheek, its cool kiss a counterpoint to the warmth of the hand that covered her own.

"Now, open them and lead us in to the shore."

She felt his hand lift away from her own and raised her gaze to the sails, gently altering their course to keep them filled. She felt exhilarated as the little boat responded to the lightest of touches.

"But this is wonderful," she said, a wide smile curving her lips.

"You are full of surprises, Miss Lockhart," he laughed.

When they reached the shore, a small wiry man with dark curling hair was waiting for them. He waded into the water and as the next incoming wave surged beneath them, pulled Betsy up onto the beach. He then held out a hand to help Katherine to alight.

"Seems as you caught a beautiful mermaid, Lord Treleven."

Katherine stepped out of the boat and smiled at him. "I could almost wish I were such a creature for then I would not have been foolish enough to have been stranded or needed rescuing from the incoming tide."

"Ah, so that was the way of it. Don't be too hard on yerself, ma'am, for you aren't the first to have been caught so and you won't be the last neither."

Lord Treleven vaulted over the side of the boat and shook the man's hand. Katherine's eyes followed his movements. She had never met a man with such vitality and natural grace, or, fortunately for her, one who had such a cool head in a crisis.

"This is Joseph Craddock," he informed her. "He taught me to sail."

Her smile widened. "Then I also find myself in your debt, Mr Craddock, for if you had not done so, Lord Treleven would not have been able to rescue me."

A slow smile spread across his weathered face. "Oh, he would have found a way, miss, of that you can be sure."

Harry nodded up the beach to where a white

cottage stood. A small wooden bench crouched against the wall.

"If you'd like to sit for a moment, Miss Lockhart, I'll just stow the boat and then I'll take you back."

Joseph helped Harry haul Betsy back up the greased planks and then helped him into his coat.

"You leave the rest to me, sir, get that lovely young lady of yours back to Elmdon. She's holding herself together well but she's had a fright and no mistake. I'm surprised she's not in hysterics truth be told."

Harry grinned at him. "I don't think Miss Lockhart is the sort to have the vapours, Joseph, she's far too sensible and dignified."

"Aye, well, off with you, anyways."

Harry nodded briefly and turned on his heels but he had gone no more than a stride when he paused and swivelled neatly again. Leaning into the boat he began gathering the scattered shells and fragments of glass. As he strode towards Joseph's cottage, he glanced at the little collection that lay in his palm. He came to a sudden stop, picked up a couple of the pieces and slid them into his coat pocket.

He paused when he reached Katherine and offered her the remainder of her treasure.

She glanced at his outstretched palm for a moment and then shook her head.

"Thank you, Lord Treleven, but let them fall. Perhaps some things are better left where they are found."

"As you wish," he said, tilting his palm so they fell to the sand.

He retrieved Hermes from the small garden behind the cottage and rode around to where Katherine now stood waiting for him.

"I am afraid I cannot trust Hermes to carry you alone, Miss Lockhart, so I will need to take you before me."

He saw a look of uncertainty cross her face and reached down his hand. "Come. There is no time for argument, Jim will have carried the tale to Elmdon by now and everyone will be concerned, I do not wish my mother, in particular, to worry any longer than necessary. Place your foot on mine and I'll do the rest."

As he now expected, sense won out over pride and she clasped his hand, rested her boot on his and sprang up before him without much aid at all.

Hermes sidled a little in protest and he firmly clasped one arm around her slender waist, feeling her stiffen as he did so, grasped the reins firmly with the other and took them home.

As soon as they entered the house, the drawing room door flew open. Lady Treleven, Henrietta, Mrs Abbott and Lord and Lady Hayward poured into the hall. They were already changed for dinner.

"Oh, thank goodness!" Lady Treleven cried coming forwards and briefly embracing her son and then Katherine. Taking a step back she gave Harry a stern look. "You are very naughty going sailing without letting anyone know what you were about! Had you forgotten Doctor Fisher was to change your dressing today?"

Katherine had not immediately perceived him but on hearing his name he stepped out from behind Lord Hayward whose huge form had obscured him from view, and offered a small bow in their direction.

"It is no matter. I can look at it as you change for dinner." His kind but penetrating gaze rested on Katherine for a moment. "I would be happy to be of service to you also, Miss Lockhart, if you feel at all unwell."

Lady Treleven took both of her hands in her own.

"Yes, do let him, dear. How terrified you must have been! I have been berating myself all afternoon for allowing you to go off on your own, but I never dreamed you would go down that steep narrow path to the beach without anyone to aid you. You must let Doctor Fisher look you over and if you do not feel up to dinner, I will have a tray sent to your room."

Katherine returned her clasp and smiled gently down at her. "It will not be necessary, as you see, I am none the worse for the experience. Please, do not blame yourself, ma'am, it was an impulsive decision, the sand looked so inviting." She glanced ruefully down at her dress. Swathes of white stained the velvet where the salt had dried against the fabric. "I cannot say the same for my gown, unfortunately, I fear it is beyond saving."

"Oh, a dress can easily be replaced, so what matter?" smiled Lady Hayward coming forwards. "And to be rescued in such a way must have been vastly exciting."

The sound of a bell ringing echoed through the large hallway. Glasson appeared as if from nowhere and glided by them with unhurried dignity.

"It appears Mr Caldwell has arrived," said Lady Treleven, beginning to usher her guests back into the drawing room.

"I must go and get changed." Katherine moved quickly towards the stairs. As she passed

Lady Hayward, she found a light hand on her arm.

"I will come with you, Miss Lockhart, for I wish to hear all about it. I wonder if I would enjoy sailing?"

"You would be horribly seasick, my dear," Lord Hayward assured her as she set her foot on the first stair. "Remember our honeymoon trip? You turned green almost as soon as we left the harbour!"

His good lady looked a trifle disappointed but sent a not unhopeful glance over her shoulder in Harry's direction. "Yes, but that was on a large ship, surely it would not be as bad on a little boat?"

"It would be worse," he assured her, grinning.

Katherine noticed the look of approval Lord Hayward cast in his direction.

"Hold the fort for me will you, Hayward?" Harry said, slipping by them and mounting the stairs two at a time. Doctor Fisher followed him at a more dignified pace.

Ayles was pacing the room when they entered her chamber. "Oh, miss!" she cried. "You have given us all such a fright! And just look at your poor gown!"

Katherine was not quite sure which was the

greater concern for her flustered maid. "Is it quite ruined?"

Ayles came forward and gently rubbed one of the stains. "Don't you worry your head over that, ma'am, there's nothing there that a good brush and a treatment of vinegar and water won't fix! Now, you wash quickly whilst I lay out a choice of gowns for you or you'll be late for dinner."

Lady Haywood smiled and sat herself on the damask covered chair that was set beneath the window. Katherine disappeared behind the screen that lay at an angle across one corner of her room and began to wash her face.

"Tell me, Miss Lockhart, is Lord Treleven as accomplished at sailing as he is at everything else?"

"As I know nothing about sailing I am hardly qualified to judge," Katherine said drily.

A tinkle of laughter greeted this. "I see you are a lady who is not easily impressed."

Feeling a twinge of guilt that she had not been more supportive of her rescuer, she added hastily, "But I certainly felt safe both in his boat and on his horse."

"He let you ride his stallion?" Lady Hayward sounded amazed.

Katherine briefly closed her eyes. She really

must learn to consider her words before she uttered them.

"Well, no," she admitted. "He took me up before him."

There was a moment's pause. "I am glad to hear it, how dreadful it would have been if you had survived one horrid ordeal only to have been thrown by that fearsome creature."

She heard a rustling of silk as if Lady Hayward had got to her feet.

"Oh, definitely that one, I think."

It seemed Lady Hayward was to choose her raiment for her. Katherine did not feel too alarmed by this development as she knew she had nothing too daring in her wardrobe.

She stepped around the screen and stared at the dress laid out on her bed. Of course, she knew she had a silk evening gown in Pomona green but she saw that the previously square cut, high neckline had been lowered and shaped, a deeper green satin ribbon had been attached below it and scalloped rouleaux of a similar green satin and blonde lace had been added to the hem of the train. She glanced at Ayles who stood with an alternating expression of hope and worry in her eyes.

She smiled. "If ever you decide to change

professions, Ayles, you will make an admirable seamstress."

When they entered the drawing room not quarter of an hour later, they found a rather awkward tableau before them. Lord Hayward sat next to Lady Treleven, whilst Henrietta and Mrs Abbott occupied the opposing sofa. Mr Gulworthy stood behind them, his hands clasped behind his back. All eyes apart from Henrietta's, whose gaze was firmly riveted to the splendid Aubusson carpet at her feet, her cheeks echoing its red tones, were fixed with amazed fascination upon Mr Caldwell who stood leaning on the mantelpiece as if he were very much at home.

As the occupants of the room registered their arrival, the eyes swivelled towards them with no small measure of relief. Lord Hayward stood and bowed before coming forwards to take his lady's hand. He took it upon himself to make the introductions, placing a slight emphasis on the words, 'my wife' when he indicated Lady Hayward.

Mr Caldwell bowed politely to this lady before turning his attentions to Katherine. She was a little startled when the rather stout man in the garish waistcoat took her hand and bowed deeply over it. She thought she heard something creak.

"I am a fortunate fellow indeed to be surrounded by such perfection."

Katherine's brows winged upwards and she retrieved her hand from his clammy grasp glad of her long gloves, but still needing to resist the almost overpowering temptation to wipe it against her gown. She was saved the necessity of making a reply by the entrance of Lord Treleven and Doctor Fisher.

"At last," Lady Treleven gave a relieved smile. "I had begun to think something was amiss. I trust the wound is healing as it should, Doctor Fisher?"

"Wound?" echoed Mr Caldwell. "Have you met with an accident, Lord Treleven? I must say you look right as a trivet to me."

"I am," Lord Treleven assured him. "It is nothing, the veriest scratch."

Katherine flushed as she remembered the exertion which he had put himself to on her behalf. She was on the point of apologising to him when he caught her eye. There was a warning there and she held her peace.

Lady Treleven advanced towards Lord Hayward. "It is time and more that we went in to dinner."

He offered her his arm and Lord Treleven proffered his to Lady Hayward.

Mr Caldwell made a move towards Henrietta and she shrank backwards, sending her mother an alarmed glance.

"Doctor Fisher, you may take my daughter in, if you please," Lady Treleven said briskly.

That young lady visibly relaxed even as Mr Caldwell frowned. Mr Gulworthy offered his escort to Mrs Abbott, leaving Katherine to Mr Caldwell. She placed her hand lightly on his forearm but he drew it within his own, giving her hand a little squeeze as he did so. Keeping her gaze firmly fixed in front of her, she suppressed a grimace.

"And who are your people, Miss Lockhart?" he enquired almost as soon as they had been seated.

"My brother is Sir Richard Lockhart of Felsham Court," she replied in a colourless tone, hoping to discourage him.

"Baronet or knight?" he shot back.

She looked at him in astonishment. "Baronet."

"And what sort of place is this Felsham Court?" he continued between mouthfuls of soup.

"I do not believe I understand you, Mr Caldwell."

"How many acres?" he clarified, undeterred by her air of frigid dignity.

"I really could not say."

He laughed, wiping a smear of soup from his chin. "Of course you cannot, and why should you? A delicate flower does not question the soil that harbours it, after all."

Her glance collided with Lady Hayward's dancing eyes and a small smile tugged at her lips.

When the ladies left the gentlemen to their port, Lady Hayward took her arm.

"I don't know how I kept my countenance. He is an extraordinary man, isn't he?"

"You almost set me off, Lady Hayward," Katherine acknowledged. "I don't know what was worse – his impertinent questions or ridiculous compliments!"

"Oh, call me Belle, please, all my friends do."

"Very well, Belle. Let us put our heads together, for we must come up with a way to keep Mr Caldwell as far away from Henrietta as possible. He will terrify and disgust her."

"You are very right," she agreed. "I often rescued her from unwanted attention when we were in town. I am afraid her rare combination of beauty and shyness might have led one or two sprigs of fashion to behave a little too warmly towards her."

Katherine paused for a moment in the hall and said in a lowered voice. "Did she tell you about Mr Carruthers?"

Belle quirked an eyebrow and a dangerous sparkle came into her eyes. "So he *did* make her faint! I always suspected as much! Imagine Mr Caldwell but fifteen years younger."

Katherine shuddered. "I think even I would have fainted!"

"Precisely. To someone of Henrietta's disposition and innocence, to be mauled by such a man must have been beyond distasteful. It makes me very angry, one's first kiss should be a magical experience, not feel like a violation!"

"Was your business in Padstow successful?" Harry smiled across at Lord Hayward.

"Oh, I may have discovered a couple of interesting leads. Mr Boodle was most helpful."

"Boodle, eh?" interjected Mr Caldwell. "Bit of an old fusspot, if you ask me. Give me a London solicitor any day. More up to snuff on some of the more, er, intricate aspects of the law, shall we say?"

"I found him to be adequate," Lord Hayward smiled sleepily. "Seems to have a good local knowledge."

"Isn't he an investor in your mine?" Harry asked.

"*Was* an investor." Mr Caldwell gave a wolfish smile. "I bought him out. He was always nitpicking over things he did not fully understand. Besides, I prefer to choose my own partners. Speaking of which, have you considered my proposal that you should become one of them?"

"I may be interested," Harry said slowly, aware that all eyes were now firmly fixed upon him with expressions varying from disinterest, surprise, and in the vicar's case, horror.

Mr Caldwell beamed. "Capital!"

"Not so fast, sir," he added. "Various conditions would have to be met."

Mr Caldwell raised a surprised brow and then laughed. "There's more to you than meets the eye, my boy. I like the cut of your jib. Come tomorrow and we will discuss it further, but I warn you, I am an old hand at negotiation!"

Lord Hayward yawned. "I find all this talk of business quite tedious. Shall we join the ladies?"

Mr Caldwell gave him an indulgent look.

"Well, we cannot all have a head for business after all. Just as well for me, eh?"

Lord Hayward gave no indication that he had heard him.

Colouring slightly, he stood up and clapped Harry on the shoulder.

"Well lead on, lead on. You have a damn fine sister, Lord Treleven, diamond of the first water. I cannot think of a pleasanter way to spend the evening than in her company! Miss Lockhart's not too shabby either, but so starched up, you'd think she was the sister of a duke rather than a mere baronet. No wonder she's been left on the shelf – who in their right mind would want to be leg-shackled to an icicle?"

It was perhaps fortunate that he turned away just at that moment or he would have witnessed the quite murderous expression that flashed in his host's eyes.

As the gentlemen entered the drawing room, Lady Treleven rang for the tea tray. Mr Caldwell drew his chair close to where Henrietta was seated, quietly conversing with Mrs Abbott. Before he could draw breath to speak, Belle turned towards him with a blinding smile.

"Mr Caldwell," she said, her eyes dropping for a moment from his florid face to his equally florid waistcoat. "You are clearly a man who knows his own taste. I feel sure you must enjoy the finer things in life."

"That I do," he concurred. "And nothing could be finer than the company in which I find myself this evening." His eyes rested hungrily on Henrietta.

"You are all kindness, sir," Belle said with a tinkle of laughter. "Such modest requirements for your entertainment are a credit to you, but you must, I think, enjoy music?"

Mr Caldwell returned her smile a little cautiously. "As much as the next man, I should think."

"I knew it," she said clapping her hands. "Then you are more fortunate than you are aware, for Miss Treleven is quite accomplished on the pianoforte, I believe."

That young lady's startled eyes shot up from the clearly fascinating pattern of the Aubusson carpet. "Oh, no, I have not prepared anything!"

Mr Caldwell looked a trifle relieved. "Please, do not trouble yourself, Miss Treleven. I am sure a little conversation is all that I require."

Henrietta blanched.

"It is an excellent idea," Lady Treleven concurred. "Come, Henrietta. There is no point developing accomplishments if you don't intend to display them."

Doctor Fisher came forwards and offered her his hand. "Don't be shy, Miss Treleven, you are amongst friends, after all. I will be happy to turn the pages for you."

She offered him a tremulous smile and got to her feet.

Mr Gulworthy took her seat and he and Mrs Abbott exchanged a friendly look. They had discovered their mutual interest in gardening during dinner and had soon established a comfortable rapport.

Despite her nerves, Henrietta managed a creditable rendition of a sonata by Haydn. She received a polite round of applause, extended by the heavy, slow clapping of Mr Caldwell, who had quickly recovered from his initial feeling of chagrin at having his quarry removed so soon from his orbit, when he had realised all the advantages of his situation. He had, in effect, been given license to sit at his ease and gaze upon her fair visage without occasioning remark or fearing interruption. If only Doctor Fisher had not leaned in quite so close as he turned the page for her, he would have been quite content. Determined that he should regain the advantage over the younger man, he rose even as he clapped and began to move towards them only to find Lady Hayward before him. She fluttered both arms in front of her, driving him back to his chair before he had taken more than a step.

"No, no, sir," she laughed. "This will not do. One piece does not an evening of entertainment make. I am sure you do not wish to deny any delicate flowers here, the opportunity to blossom."

Her eyes turned to Katherine on the words. "Perhaps you could sing for us, Miss Lockhart?"

"If you wish," she smiled, swiftly crossing to Henrietta who had begun to rise. "You play and I'll sing, if you please, Miss Treleven, for I am afraid I have not applied myself to the instrument for some years now."

Henrietta sank back on her stool.

Picking up a songbook, Katherine began to flick through it. A loose sheet of music floated to the floor. She made to retrieve it but Lord Treleven was before her. He glanced at it for a moment and then smiled, a mischievous glint in his eye.

"Do you know 'From Night 'til Morn I take my Glass', Miss Lockhart? It was one of my father's favourites."

"I do, but—" Katherine glanced over to her hostess, unsure if she would approve of such a lively song about drowning one's sorrows to forget a past love.

Lady Treleven considered Mr Caldwell for a moment. "I am sure it will go down very well, Miss Lockhart. Harry, you must join in also for it is meant as a duet, after all."

Harry glanced at his sister and she gave him a small smile and a nod of her head. Their voices blended perfectly, Harry effortlessly finding a counter melody and Katherine matching his tempo, and, in the end, his enjoyment.

The room erupted into laughter and applause as they finished. Mr Caldwell beaming as broadly as any of them.

Harry took Katherine's hand and bowed over it, his twinkling gaze never leaving her own.

"You sing as sweetly as a nightingale," he murmured.

Even as she felt the heat rush up her arm and into her cheeks, she perceived over his shoulder Mr Caldwell again determined to approach. His eyes were only for Henrietta so when she moved very close to him, he did not immediately perceive that the train of her dress was in his path. Sending a silent apology to Ayles, she timed her moment to perfection, moving away at the very moment his heavy tread encountered her gown. The sound of tearing reached every ear.

Mr Caldwell reddened. "Miss Lockhart, forgive me. I do not know how such a thing could have happened!"

Katherine smiled graciously. "Do not disturb yourself, Mr Caldwell, I am sure it will take but a moment to pin it up." She turned to Henrietta. "Would you mind very much lending me a hand, Miss Treleven?"

"Of course, Miss Lockhart, please, come with me." She glided gracefully to the door, Katherine following in her wake, determinedly keeping her gaze far from Belle.

Barely had the door shut behind them before Henrietta covered her face in her hands. Katherine looked at her in surprise. She could not see any cause for her distress.

"Miss Treleven, Henrietta," she began, concerned, but came to an abrupt halt as Henrietta let her hands fall, to reveal two eyes that were shining with laughter, not tears.

"You guessed?" she gasped, surprised.

Henrietta nodded. "Did you not say that mice were observant creatures, Miss Lockhart?"

"Katherine," she smiled. "Indeed I did. But I may have failed to mention that they can at times be quite forgetful. It may take you some time to lay your hands on those pins!"

CHAPTER 9

When Harry went down to the stables the next morning, he found Lord Hayward there.

"Morning, Hayward. Where are you off to this morning?"

"I thought I'd ride towards Hayle."

Harry looked surprised. "I would have thought Penzance would be a better bet. There are some fine houses in South Parade."

"I am sure you are right, but I fancied a coastal ride this morning."

Harry nodded briskly and mounted Hermes. "Then we'll ride together awhile. I'll take a closer look at Caldwell's set-up before I go and see him."

"Mr Gulworthy did not seem to approve of your interest in his mine," he mused.

Harry sighed. "He will when he understands that it may be the only way I can influence who is employed there. Many local hardworking men and women have lost out to the people Caldwell has brought in."

"I would not have thought it would have been worth his while," Lord Hayward murmured.

Harry gave him a close look, surprised that he was prepared to discuss a subject that had been so distasteful to him only the evening before.

"That thought has also crossed my mind," Harry admitted.

"And have you come up with any likely explanations?" Lord Hayward gently pressed.

Harry looked thoughtful. "Not likely ones, no, so if you don't mind, Hayward, I'll keep my thoughts to myself for now. I don't like to cast aspersions on a man's character before I have firm evidence to go on."

Lord Hayward smiled his sleepy smile. "Very admirable, Treleven. Miss Lockhart and my esteemed wife, seem already to have formed some firm conclusions on his character, however."

Harry's countenance lightened as he

grinned. "I almost felt sorry for him. They thwarted him at every turn."

"Their performance was indeed masterful but their motives were, I think, to be applauded."

"That is why I said, 'almost'. It was not until he trod upon Miss Lockhart's gown that I saw their game. I really am very grateful to them for he would have overwhelmed Henrietta and in all likelihood, angered me."

"Quite so," Lord Hayward agreed. "Doctor Fisher handled himself well, I thought. Comes from a very good family, you know."

"Yes, he is related to Gulworthy, who is, if memory serves me correctly, a brother-in-law of the Earl of Gantray."

Hayward nodded. "Doctor Fisher is Gantray's son. I know his older brother, Gerald, quite well. It seems the earl withdrew any form of support from Fisher when he decided on a medical profession rather than going into the church."

"That seems rather harsh," Harry replied. "His profession is perhaps not quite as esteemed as the church or the law, but it is quite re-spectable, after all."

"Gantray does not like to have his will crossed."

They were approaching the mine and picked their way around heaps of spoil. The draughty sheds, which should have been occupied by busy bal maidens hammering the copper ore, were deserted. The reason soon became clear. A crowd had gathered further down the slope towards the cliff and faint moans and chatter drifted towards them on the breeze. Dismounting, they led their horses towards the commotion. Snippets of conversation reached their ears.

"Where is it all going to end?"

"He won't be happy 'til we've paid him twice over, in blood!"

"He'll lose that leg, you mark my words!"

As they drew closer, a keening moan soared above the rest. They found Doctor Fisher kneeling by an unconscious man, a woman stood by his side. She had torn the bonnet from her head and was kneading it in her hands. Tears poured unchecked down her face as she moaned her distress.

The man's trousers were muddied and torn revealing a mangled mess of blood and bone. A rough stretcher made of wood and sack lay next to him and at a nod from the doctor, two men stepped forwards and positioned it close to the injured man. Doctor

Fisher swiftly bound his legs together at thigh and ankle and then rolled the man onto his side. The stretcher was pushed beneath the body and the doctor gently rolled him back down. As he stood and turned, Harry stepped forwards.

"What has happened here?"

"Lord Treleven! Good morning. Poor chap fell down one of the ladders, bashed his leg on sharp outcrops of rock all the way down apparently. It is a mercy he has not yet regained consciousness."

Suddenly, a pinch-faced man erupted into the crowd, waving his hands at the women and children who had downed tools to take a closer look. "Get back to work! This is not a circus! Anyone still here in the next thirty seconds will have their wages docked!"

The crowd scattered like leaves blown in the wind.

The man turned to look enquiringly at Harry and Lord Hayward. "Mr Scorrier," he informed them. "Anything I can do for you gentlemen?"

"We were just passing," Harry said, frowning. "Does this sort of thing happen often here, Scorrier?"

"Mining's a dangerous business, sir. Accidents are bound to happen no matter how careful you are."

The men with the stretcher had begun moving towards a little row of cottages on the other side of the workings.

"Gentlemen." The doctor bowed and made to follow them.

Harry laid a restraining hand on his arm. He had seen enough wounds in his time to know when a leg could not be saved. "Anything I can do, Fisher?"

Harry thought he saw something like surprise in his eyes. "Thank you, but those two should suffice." He nodded to the two stretcher-bearers and offered a rather grim smile. "I came here to gain experience and offer my help to those who really need it. It seems both aims are to be achieved today. I cannot save the leg but let us hope I can save the man."

"Oi! You little rat, what have you there?"

Harry turned to see what had occasioned such outrage in Mr Scorrier. Lord Hayward was bent over a rather grimy little girl, her twig-thin arm grasped in his huge hand. She looked terrified and two large, silent tears traced their way through the dust that smeared her face.

"You thievin' varmint." Mr Scorrier raised a hand as if to strike the girl.

"Desist!"

Harry had never before heard that tone from Lord Hayward. It stopped the man in his tracks. In softer tones he added, "You are mistaken, fellow. This young lady is rather to be commended for returning the purse that I had carelessly dropped."

He held it up. "See, the string has broken." Opening it, he withdrew a few coins and taking the girls fist, opened it and dropped them there.

She looked at him for a moment as if he had lost his mind, eyes wide, and then turned and ran before he could change it.

He turned back to Mr Scorrier, a frown between his brows. "Is it really necessary to employ children at so tender an age?"

"We need them for the picking, sir."

"Picking?"

"Yes, sir. Separating the small bits of copper ore from the waste. Takes keen sight and nimble fingers."

Lord Hayward looked sceptical. "That one didn't look like she's had a good meal in a long time."

Mr Scorrier shrugged. "We pay 'em tokens so they can buy their food from us. Encourages them not to drink it away. There's not much more we can do."

"Tokens? You do not even give them coin for their back-breaking labour?"

Not waiting for the inevitable excuses, he mounted his horse. As they rode back up the slope, he turned to Harry.

"If the goods they are allowed to purchase for their 'tokens' are not inferior in quality and overinflated in price, you may call me a moon-ling! No wonder she tried to filch my purse."

He seethed with an indignation that was very much at odds with his usual air of placidity. They paused as a pack of mules carrying heavy sacks of ore plodded past them.

"I would not be at all surprised if you are right," Harry acknowledged. "One mystery, at least, becomes a little clearer, however. There is no way our men would have agreed to such a system!"

"*One* mystery?" Lord Hayward said softly. "May I enquire as to what the other might be?"

Harry shook his head. "It is all conjecture at the moment."

They had come to a small road. "Our ways part here," Harry said.

Lord Hayward nodded. "Be careful how you tread with Caldwell."

Harry raised a brow.

"You may or may not find yourself in a position to improve conditions here if you have a stake in the mine. Either way, I think you will find he will demand a higher price than you are prepared to pay. It might be worth your while to stall him if this occurs rather than turn him down outright."

Harry watched him ride off. He rarely underestimated his man but it suddenly dawned on him that he had been duped into believing Hayward a bit of a slow top. He had thought he and Belle were something of a mismatch but now a few things began to fall into place. The way he had steered her away from begging an invitation to go sailing came to mind, and the way a smiling look accompanied by a slightly raised eyebrow had silenced her once or twice at dinner. He undoubtedly held her on a light rein, but hold her he did.

This was not the only point on which his judgement had been at fault. Whilst it was natural that his sympathies should have been focused on his own people, he had hardly spared a thought for Caldwell's workers. He had condemned them out of hand. He was now inclined to think they were just as much victims of Caldwell's manipulation. The poor souls he had seen today had looked ragged and miserable. The likelihood was that they were hopelessly in his debt.

When he informed Caldwell of what he had seen that day, the man showed not a glimmer of concern.

"Come, come, sir," he said. "The accident was unfortunate but not unusual. There is no place for sentiment in business."

Even as he felt his ire rise, he remembered Hayward's words and damped it down.

"Perhaps so, sir. But I have been brought up to consider the wellbeing of my dependents."

Caldwell suddenly smiled. "Well, my boy, if you decide to join with me, there may be some room for negotiation, after all."

"There would have to be," Harry said shortly. "I would require at a very minimum that some of those who lost their jobs would be re-employed and paid *in coin* a fair amount for their labour and ore. I would also like to call in an independent expert to assess the safety of the mine and would need assurances that any shortcomings would be swiftly and thoroughly addressed."

Mr Caldwell looked slightly taken aback and not best pleased by this list of requirements. His colour heightened even as his eyes narrowed.

"You are full of demands, Lord Treleven,

but I think you will find negotiation is a two-way process."

"I am listening," Harry said.

Mr Caldwell relaxed back in his chair and steepled his fingers, a conciliatory smile curving his lips. "It is not outside the realms of probability that I might accede to some or even all of your requests," he admitted.

Harry let out a long, slow breath.

"And as you are so concerned with the well-being of your dependents, I hope my proposal will find favour with you."

Harry waited with barely restrained impatience as Caldwell stood and poured out two glasses of claret. He passed one to him before perching on the edge of his desk.

"Yes, on reflection, I think I might be amenable to all of your demands if you will but agree to support my claim to your lovely sister's hand in marriage. I told you, did I not, that I wished to settle down? Turn respectable if you will."

Harry's brows shot up. The very thought of his gentle, shy sister being aligned with Caldwell was anathema to him. Hayward's words of warning were forgotten as he surged to his feet. "Never!"

A slightly ugly look came over his host's face.

"Never is a long time, Lord Treleven. Fortunes change, sometimes for the worse. Would it not be better to secure a comfortable and safe future for Miss Treleven, now, whilst you still have something to bargain with?"

Harry carefully put down the untouched glass of claret and surveyed his host coolly.

"I do not think you would suit, sir," he said with icy politeness. "Neither do I think we could ever do business together. It is not a fine house or a gently bred wife that makes a gentleman, Mr Caldwell. Good day."

Even though he had lost his opportunity to influence the mine owner, he could not regret his words. He was not prepared to even pretend to barter with his sister as collateral. If he had done so he would have had to ask Henrietta to play along, forcing her into the man's company. It would have caused her much distress and he doubted very much she would have been able to carry it off.

Although he did not much feel like it, he decided he must make the overdue call on Mr Treen on the way home. Knowing it was much quicker to cross the fields rather than navigate the maze of narrow, deep-set lanes, he unlatched a gate and left the road. He racked his brains to try and find another way to put pressure on

Caldwell. There was none, of course. Then he recalled the conversation about Boodle. He had allowed Caldwell to buy him out and would know of any other investors, perhaps they could be persuaded to bring some pressure to bear on him.

Lost in his thoughts, he did not see the sudden dip in the ground that made Hermes stumble. Instinct came to his rescue. He raised the reins and leant back in the saddle, easing the weight on his horse's shoulders and allowing him to recover. His mount seemed unsettled by the incident, so he dismounted and went to his head. Stroking his muzzle gently, he calmed him with a string of softly uttered words. He was, he realised, standing in a large saucer shaped dip. The grass had been disrupted by wide cracks that ran through the soil.

"Lord Treleven, sir!"

He turned to see a ruddy-faced man striding purposefully towards him. Leading Hermes, he went to meet him.

"Good morning, Mr Treen. I had meant to come to you yesterday, but something else came up."

"I never expected you to come yourself, sir. Very good of you it is. And to think you nearly took a tumble for your troubles."

Harry grinned at him. "My own fault, I wasn't paying attention."

"To be honest, milord, I'm surprised as your horse stepped a foot in that dip. It appeared a few weeks ago and my sheep won't go anywhere near it." He shook his head. "Danged if I can explain it."

Having decided to take a trip to Padstow to visit Mr Boodle, he had little desire to discuss the vagaries of Mr Treen's sheep. "Well, never mind. Perhaps you *can* explain the matters which require attention?" Harry said gently.

"Oh, yes, well it's nothing too serious, sir. Some of the fencing needs redoing, some of my sheep got out and it was a right old job to round them up again. Come this way, sir."

Thoroughly enjoying having her son within her orbit again, Belle decided to take him to see the boats in the harbour at Padstow. Katherine and Henrietta accompanied her. Edmund clapped and wriggled in Belle's arms as they went down to the harbour. Several fishing boats were tied up together, and one larger, tall-masted ship towered regally above them.

They descended from the barouche and

began to walk along the quay, the little boy held in a firm grip by Belle on one side and Henrietta on the other. They laughed as he tried to drag them forwards, clearly not comprehending why anyone would walk when it was possible to run. They passed a set of steps that led onto a narrow stretch of sand. A woman sat on each of the top three steps, each wrapped in warm woollen shawls. They were busy gutting fish. One turned a lined face and gave the boy a toothless grin. Edmund gave her a wide smile.

"Are they slipp'ry?" he asked.

The woman gave a throaty laugh. "Ain't you 'andsome? Come and feel for yourself."

She held out the fish but Belle shook her head. "Thank you, my good lady, another time perhaps."

"I want to feel the fish!" Edmund complained as she dragged him along the quay.

Henrietta squatted beside him, pointing down to the sand. "What do you think they are doing?"

Two men were wielding axes, slowly revealing a huge timber beam that lay hidden beneath several layers of barnacles.

The little boy strained to be free, clearly wanting to join in. "Let me go! Let me go!"

Katherine, who stood a little behind the others, felt a light hand on her arm. She turned her head and looked straight into the amused eyes of Lord Treleven. For some strange reason, she felt a blush steal over her cheeks. He winked and took a step forwards.

"Edmund, gentlemen do not whine!"

The boy's head snapped around at this authoritative utterance, his grey eyes huge and considering.

"Harry!" Henrietta smiled, rising to her feet.

He nodded and took her place beside Edmund. "It is probably from an old wreck," he explained.

"What's wreck?"

Harry pointed to the large boat. "See that ship?"

Edmund nodded enthusiastically.

"It's made from lots of pieces of wood, like that one. But sometimes the big ships fall to the bottom of the sea."

The little boys eyes widened. "They get covered in barnacles. That's what the men are removing with their axes."

Harry grinned at the little boy. "Would you like to go on that big ship?"

Edmund looked unsure. "Will it sink to the bottom of the sea?"

Harry laughed. "No, it will not, I assure you."

"Take me on the ship!"

Harry gave him a stern look.

"Please."

"I think you should apologise to the ladies first, don't you?"

Edmund turned solemnly and bowed. "I apol'gise."

Harry cast Belle an enquiring glance. As she smiled and nodded, he hoisted her son onto his shoulders. "I will meet you in The White Hart Inn, ladies."

They turned and made their way towards the town, past the tall three-storey customs house. They came to a small square, several narrow cobbled streets, crammed with houses leading off from it. It was market day and the space was filled with stalls selling everything from fish, fruit, and pies, to pots, pans, bonnets or fine examples of bone lace.

They paused at one that had an array of wooden toys.

"Oh, look at how skilfully made this is," Belle exclaimed, holding up a model of a three-masted ship. "I must have it for Edmund."

"It is indeed exquisite," agreed Katherine, considering the delicate masts. "But do you think it will withstand his enthusiastic attentions?"

Belle laughed. "You are right, it would probably not last the day."

Katherine picked up a more sturdy looking fishing boat and raised a brow.

"Not as pretty," Belle said a little regretfully, "but far more sensible."

"Miss Treleven! Miss Treleven!"

They turned to see two ladies approaching. One was young, tall and slender, with vibrant bright red locks peeping from beneath her bonnet, the other older, shorter, and quite stout. Her hair was also red, but had sadly faded.

"Lady Humphrey, Miss Humphrey," Henrietta nodded politely before introducing her friends.

"I was wondering why you had not returned our visit." Lady Humphrey's smile did not quite reach her eyes. "But as I now realise you have guests, I shall forgive the slight."

Henrietta coloured. "No slight was intended, ma'am, I assure you. We have many calls to make, but as yet we have had no time."

"Oh, what is it you have there?" said Miss Humphrey, eyeing the toy Lady Hayward held.

As it was quite clear what she had, Belle did not answer but held up the little boat.

"How quaint," Miss Humphrey continued, "and how *kind* of you to purchase something so crudely carved." She turned to Henrietta. "Is your brother with you today?"

"Yes," said Henrietta. "He is to meet us at The White Hart Inn."

Miss Humphrey's lips opened on a smile, revealing a set of very yellow teeth. It was a shame as, apart from that one imperfection, she really was quite beautiful.

"Oh, how splendid," she twittered, linking her arm with Henrietta's. "We will accompany you if you don't mind, for I, for one, am quite, quite parched."

Belle and Katherine exchanged knowing glances and fell in behind them as they threaded through the mass of people.

"It is strange, is it not," murmured Belle, "how shopping can make one quite suddenly so very thirsty?"

Katherine bit her lip.

"So," Lady Humphrey said, almost as soon as they were seated. "How did you find your season, Miss Treleven? I would have asked when we called on you, but I am afraid with all the excitement of the return of your brother, it quite slipped my mind. I assume you did not catch an eligible bachelor? I am sure your mother must have mentioned it if you had indeed been so fortunate."

"No, ma'am," Henrietta confirmed quietly.

Miss Humphrey tittered. "Oh, but then you have never been very good at putting yourself forwards, have you?"

"I have never understood why some girls seem to think it so important to make a match when they are only just out," said Belle. 'It would be so dull to enjoy only one season before one settled down, don't you think?"

Lady Humphrey's suddenly narrowed eyes seemed to suggest that she did not agree.

"I often saw Miss Treleven positively engulfed by admirers," she continued. "I must say, I thought she displayed very good judgement not to make so important a choice so quickly, for I have seen some quite disastrous results when unions are made in such a scrambling way."

"A young lady should not be required to make any such judgement," Lady Humphrey said. "That is what her parents, or in this case, parent, is for. Do not tell me, Lady Hayward, that your own did not influence your choice."

Belle smiled, but her eyes glittered in a way that would have made any of her family, if they had been present, very wary.

"As it happens, Lady Humphrey, they did

not. I had accepted an offer before they knew anything about it."

"Well!" Lady Humphrey said, her tone dripping with disapproval.

Belle smiled widely at her. "Do not look so shocked, ma'am. Their faith in my judgement was not misplaced. They thoroughly approve of my husband and I could not be happier. But, enough about me." She turned to Miss Humphrey, her eyes dwelling for a moment on her gown, which was not of the latest fashion. "I do not think I saw you in town, did you not come up for the season?"

Katherine felt it was time to step in. Although she understood Belle's desire to protect her friend, she could not help feeling some sympathy for Miss Humphrey, who had turned an interesting shade of pink, the colour unfortunately clashing with her lovely hair.

"I have not enjoyed a season myself," she smiled. "I expect you have some local assemblies that you attend?"

The young lady pouted. "Yes, of course, but they are sadly flat."

Her gaze suddenly shifted over Katherine's shoulder and her rather sour expression was suddenly transformed.

"Lord Treleven!" she exclaimed. "Who have

you there? I declare, that sweet little boy could almost be your son!"

Katherine could not disagree. Apart from anything else he appeared quite at home handling a child so young. Edmund had been giggling as they entered the room and Lord Treleven's eyes were alight with laughter, but they lost some of their sparkle when he perceived the company.

Harry placed Edmund carefully on the floor and bowed politely. "I can assure you, ma'am, that he is not."

Edmund ran to his mama. Belle scooped him up and offered him the toy boat.

Miss Humphrey gave a trill of laughter. "Well, how could he be? But never mind that, we have just been saying how dull the local assemblies are, Lord Treleven, and seeing you has put me in mind of something."

"Indeed, Miss Humphrey?"

"I have often heard that your father used to hold the most splendid Michaelmas balls. Isn't that so, Mama?"

"Indeed it is. What a good idea, child. Miss Treleven was just saying how many visits she and her mama need to make – it would be the perfect solution."

Miss Humphrey clapped excitedly. "Oh,

please say you will, sir. I vow I will expire with disappointment, if you don't!"

Katherine could see by the sudden stiffening of his posture that he was not overly enamoured with this idea.

"Although I would not wish to be the cause of so calamitous an event, Miss Humphrey, I am not at all sure my mother will be able to commit to such a vast undertaking at the present moment."

The pout appeared again.

"Nonsense," Belle said lightly. She considered Henrietta for a moment and then smiled. "I think it a splendid idea. You should at least put the suggestion forward, Lord Treleven. She has, after all, many hands more than willing and able to help her."

CHAPTER 10

Any hope that he might harbour that his mother would veto the proposal was quickly snuffed out at dinner that evening.

"Although I hesitate to satisfy such an impertinent request, coming as it does from a young lady I consider very coming and lacking altogether in modesty or manners, the idea does have some merit." She held up her hand before Harry could protest. "We do indeed owe several persons a visit, as do you I suspect. On top of this, we would not only provide entertainment for our guests, but Henrietta would, I feel sure, be more comfortable at a ball held in her own home than she did when surrounded by strangers in town. Besides all this, I feel some sort of celebration to mark your homecoming is in order."

Harry, driven to the last ditch, looked to his sister for support.

"You cannot wish for it, Henrietta."

His sister glanced at the other ladies seated around the table, and received an encouraging look from them all.

"I think I might," she said slowly. "Could we invite Doctor Fisher? He makes me feel at ease, if I could dance with him first I would feel braver, I think."

"Bravo," Katherine said gently.

Harry's surprised gaze fell upon her. "Do not tell me that you wish to dance until dawn, Miss Lockhart?"

If timid Henrietta could overcome her fears, Katherine was determined she would match her. She would not only attend the ball, she would enjoy every moment of it!

"I love to dance," she informed him.

She looked over at Lady Treleven. "Please say you will let me help organise it. I would so enjoy it."

"Of course you would," Harry murmured.

Lady Treleven gave no sign she had heard her son. "I would be very grateful for the assistance." She glanced down the table. "You gentlemen may entertain yourselves this evening, we ladies have a lot of details to discuss, which you would find quite tedious."

Harry turned to Lord Hayward as soon as they left the room.

"Let us retire to my study, we will be both more private and more comfortable."

When they were both settled with a brandy, Harry gave his guest a very direct look.

"I think it is time we stopped fencing with each other, Hayward."

That gentleman turned his sleepy gaze upon Harry and raised an enquiring brow.

"Stop trying to play the slow-top," he said briskly. "I have realised there is nothing much that passes you by. Furthermore, if you came down here to look for a property, then it is I who am the moonling!"

Lord Hayward dropped the act. His eyes sharpened. "I must be losing my touch. What is it that gave me away?"

"Your words of advice for a start. You were quite correct. Caldwell did demand too high a price."

Lord Hayward looked pensive. "And did you take my advice?"

Harry shrugged. "I tried at first, but I could not play with Henrietta as the bargaining chip."

"It is a pity," Lord Hayward sighed. "But I suspected as much."

"And then I visited Boodle today."

"Ah," Lord Hayward said with his customary calm. "Anything else?"

"Yes," confirmed Harry. "Whilst entertaining your son upon the Lady Lucy, which is at present docked in Padstow harbour, I met an old colleague of mine."

"Really?"

"Yes, a military gentleman. He was unfortunately quite vague about why his regiment were visiting."

"I commend his discretion," Lord Hayward murmured.

"Damn his discretion. What interest do you have in Caldwell?" he asked. "Be frank, man!"

"Ah, now we come to it," he said thoughtfully. "You must forgive my reticence to confide in you, Treleven."

"Must I?" Harry said tersely.

Lord Hayward smiled. "Yes, I really think you must. Although my wife spoke highly of you, and in general she is a good judge of character, I felt in this case, I could not trust her instinct alone. I'm afraid I was not convinced you were to be trusted in this *particular* matter."

"Why ever not?" Harry said, exasperated.

"Your reputation goes before you," Lord Hayward said briefly.

"My reputation? If you refer to my duel, I cannot think what bearing it might have on anything."

"No, no. Your duel was unfortunate, but it was what came afterwards that concerned me."

Harry's eyes narrowed. "What do you know about what came afterwards?"

"I believe you were involved in, shall we say, some illicit dealings?"

"How the devil would you know that?" Harry demanded.

"Lloyd's Coffee House," Lord Hayward said. "I do not know if you are aware of the fact, but most men interested in ships and their insurance gather there."

"And?" said Harry.

"And, Treleven, they base their speculation on the reputation of the ship owners and captains. Lloyd's have agents in ports around the world. They have been very useful to us in many ways. And sometimes they report things that might be of interest to certain of our agents. We were aware that you were operating between Europe and America."

"Were you, by God? And who, exactly, is we?"

"The government in times of war and certain members of it, who have invested heavily in shipping, at other times."

Harry began to see the light.

"Has this something to do with the wreck?"

"Indeed it does. It was an East Indiaman. It was carrying a very valuable cargo."

"But if it was insured, why this cloak and dagger investigation?"

"The usual channels were employed at first, of course. They turned up nothing. The insurers are not satisfied in this case. And then there is the king."

Harry looked startled.

"He also had an interest in this particular cargo. He had procured a number of jewels. In particular, a very rare and large sapphire, which cannot be easily replaced."

"He always has had a taste for the exotic," Harry acknowledged. "But why suspect Caldwell?"

"He had for many years a good reputation as a sound businessman. But he has himself lost two ships in the last year, both of which were heavily insured. There were suggestions that both ships veered from the usual route but he was given the benefit of the doubt on both occasions. However, the captain of the wrecked Indiaman used to work for him. It may be coincidence that the ship was lost so close to his new residence or it might not. But it has occurred to me that if something smoky is going on, and if he has something to hide, he has miles of underground tunnels which might come in very handy for the purpose."

"And you thought I might be a part of it?" Harry said, disgusted.

"Hardly," Lord Hayward said gently, "but perhaps sympathetic enough to turn a blind eye? Cornwall is renowned for smuggling and wrecking, after all. Very few of the salvaged goods from a wrecked ship are given over to the customs officer, after all, even though those who have them, may claim salvage."

"Intentionally wrecking a ship and harvesting goods washed up on the beach are two very different things. I know no wreckers. And you must be aware that it can take years for a salvage claim to be paid, if it is at all! The government cannot expect the poor and hungry to follow their system until they make it fair!"

"I sympathise," Lord Hayward said. "But if we all ignored the law when it did not suit, there would be anarchy. But you perhaps begin to see why I did not, at first, fully trust you in this matter?"

Harry was a fair man. He could see his point. "I suppose I do," he conceded.

"That has, however, ceased to be the case," Lord Hayward informed him, smiling. "As a matter of fact, I hope that we can work together. Our interests are now aligned, for I am sure you would like nothing better than for Caldwell to be removed from your vicinity."

"Wouldn't I just," Harry muttered.

Lord Hayward stood and held out his hand. "Let's shake on it."

Never one to bear a grudge for long, Harry shook his hand and smiled.

"You're a dark horse, Hayward. I think I may have something that will be of interest to you." He strolled across to his desk, opened a drawer and withdrew a small velvet pouch. He threw it over to Lord Hayward.

Catching it deftly in one hand, he tipped its contents into his huge palm. He glanced quickly up at Harry before reaching for his quizzing glass and examining them carefully.

"If I am not very much mistaken, Treleven, I have here a ruby and a rather fine diamond. Do you mind me asking where you acquired them?"

"Not at all. Miss Lockhart found them, on the beach below Caldwell's mine. She thought them bits of glass."

"And did you correct her misapprehension?" Lord Hayward enquired.

Harry shook his head. "No. I wanted time to work through my suspicions. They seemed outrageous, fantastical even. But I was uneasy about the wreck, there was wild talk of Caldwell's miners having harvested the goods and even of having caused it. Yet there was no evidence to implicate them, until those two little beauties turned up." He frowned. "I still don't think I believe it. He keeps his workers in abject poverty, treats them little better than slaves, I cannot think he would trust them with something that could ruin him. They can have no love for the man, after all."

"No," mused Lord Hayward. "I suppose it is not outside the realms of possibility that they were washed up on the shore. I certainly need more to go on if I am to apply to the local magistrate for the power of search and seizure."

"It may be within the realms of possibility, but not, I think, probability." Harry grinned at him.

"Go on."

"They were found very close to an adit that should have been pouring water after hours of heavy rain, yet was not."

A wide smile slowly spread across Lord Hayward's face. "I think we have him, Treleven. I think we have him."

"There may be a conflict of interest there, I'm afraid," warned Harry. "The local magistrate is Lord Humphrey. He is also the only other investor in the mine."

"I am aware," Lord Hayward informed him. "But from what I have been able to discover, he leaves it all to Caldwell. I think you will find that he will very quickly distance himself from the man and help in any way he can in order to exonerate himself from any culpability in the matter."

CHAPTER 11

The following day dawned overcast but dry. At breakfast, Katherine announced she was going to drive over to Helagon to see Mrs Nance.

"Would you like me to come with you, my dear?" enquired Mrs Abbott. "I am quite happy to although I was going to plan the flower arrangements for the ball."

"There is no need," Katherine said. "I wish to see if Mrs Nance would be willing to lend Mrs Kemp a hand with some of the preparations."

"That is a very good idea, Miss Lockhart," Lady Treleven said approvingly. "And it is very kind of you to think of it."

"I will aid you with the writing of the invitations," smiled Belle. "I don't suppose there will be time to send them to the printers."

"No," agreed Lady Treleven. "The moon will be full at the end of next week, so we cannot put it off."

"I will come with you," Harry said suddenly to Katherine. "I wish to have a word with Mr Hewel and I think I will find him there."

"As you wish," Katherine said. She glanced a little wistfully out of the window at the rolling parkland beyond.

"Do you drive or ride?" she asked after a few moments.

"Ride. Hermes requires a considerable amount of exercise but stubbornly refuses to let anyone else mount him."

"I wonder," she began, and then hesitated.

Harry raised a brow. "What is it you wonder, Miss Lockhart?"

She looked a little bashful. "Would it be terribly rude of me, if I asked to borrow a horse? It seems an age since I have enjoyed a gallop."

He smiled at her. "Not at all. I'll meet you at the stables in half an hour, and you may take your pick of the few that we have."

He was amply rewarded by the wide, warm smile bestowed upon him.

Katherine hurried into her close-fitting pale

blue riding habit; it was an old friend and severe in style. She had strictly forbidden Ayles to tamper with it in any way and raised a stern eyebrow when she regarded her habit shirt.

"Oh, it is only a bit of lace I've added to the collar," she said, as she finished tying the soft muslin cravat in a neat bow. "There's nothing wrong with a bit of—"

"Prettifying," Katherine finished for her. "I know, Ayles."

When she arrived at the stables, Lord Treleven was speaking to Lord Hayward who was already mounted. He touched his hand to his hat and smiled, before trotting off.

"Where is he off to today?" asked Katherine.

"Oh, here and there," said Harry vaguely. "I am afraid our stable is not what it once was, Miss Lockhart."

Kenver nodded politely as they entered and touched his cap. "I was thinking you might like to take out Misty, ma'am," he said, indicating a placid looking mare. "She's Miss Treleven's horse and has a very nice temper."

"Perhaps," Katherine murmured, walking on until she came to the last stall. Here she found a bay mare of about sixteen hands. She looked powerful, her neck arched nicely and she had a proud bearing.

"This one, I think," Katherine smiled. "She has quality."

Kenver gave a short laugh. "She may have quality but she also has the devil's own temper, ma'am. We call her Countess, for she's very demanding and likes her own way!"

"That does not mean she has to have it." Katherine glanced at Lord Treleven. "You did say, sir, that I might choose?"

"By all means," he said and then suddenly grinned. "Perhaps I should fetch a flask of brandy in case you take a tumble, Miss Lockhart."

Katherine smiled at his sally, remembering their first meeting. "I doubt very much it will be necessary."

The mare behaved well enough as she mounted her, but as soon as she took the reins in her hands she snorted and reared. Katherine did not panic, but kept her weight well forwards and her hands soft. As soon as all four hooves were firmly on the floor again, she stroked her neck and murmured to her.

"There, Countess, you're eager for a run, as am I, but there is no need for these manners."

Kenver and Harry exchanged a look of approval.

"We will take a ride through the park," Harry said. "I usually do every morning, and we can cut cross country to Helagon."

"As you wish."

After a few minor skirmishes, Countess discovered that Katherine was ready for all her tricks and settled down recognising the skill and confidence of her rider.

"My compliments," Harry smiled. "I have only ever seen one other lady with such a fine seat."

"Oh? And who was that?" Katherine enquired.

"Lady Bray, who has just married my friend, Sir Philip Bray. You would like her, I think."

"Then I must hope to make her acquaintance," Katherine said.

"If you settle here, you no doubt will. They are bound to visit me some time or other. I would have invited them to our ball if they were not so newly wed."

"You have resigned yourself to it, then?"

He gave a short laugh. "I was outnumbered and outgunned! I did not object on principle but I would have preferred it to be nearer to Christmas, I must admit. I have a lot on my mind at the moment."

Katherine would have liked to know what was troubling him, but she did not ask as she was enjoying his company and did not wish to risk being rebuffed.

A long, flat expanse of grass stretched out before them. Harry met her gaze and quirked a brow. "Shall we?"

Katherine answered by touching her heel lightly to Countess's side and moving smoothly into a canter. She felt a smile stretch across her face as they switched to a gallop her mount proving as swift as she had hoped. She exchanged a smiling glance with Lord Treleven who easily matched her pace and noted the sparkle in his eyes, realising he was enjoying this just as much as she. They gradually slowed as they neared a flock of sheep that were grazing nearby.

"It is good to see you enjoying yourself, Miss Lockhart. The exercise has put a bloom in your cheeks. It suits you."

"I used to ride out every day at home," she said a little wistfully.

"Do you miss it very much?" Harry enquired gently.

Katherine put on a brave smile. "Do not encourage me in melancholy reflections, sir," she said briskly. "I am sure I will grow very fond of Helagon once I become accustomed to it. It is just that it is a little strange to feel," she paused as if searching for the right words, "oh, I don't know, a little lost, I suppose."

"It is completely understandable, Miss Lockhart." His gaze drifted off into the middle distance for a moment as if his thoughts were far away. "No one understands that feeling more than I," he said softly. "You have lost your anchor and are drifting with the tide."

"Yes, that is exactly it," she said quietly.

Harry's gaze refocused, the lurking laughter that was so often present, apparent again. "Tell me about this harpy who has driven you out."

Katherine laughed. "I would not call her a harpy!"

"No, I will not have it. She is a harpy, I am quite sure of it!"

"I will not say so," Katherine said. "She is just a little irritable, shall we say. But then she is in the family way so I am sure it is quite understandable."

"So is Belle in the family way," he pointed out. "And I would not describe her as irritable."

"No, she is delightful," Katherine smiled.

"I agree," Harry said. "As are you."

Their eyes met, Katherine's widening in surprise at the compliment, which somehow felt quite genuine. Her heart began to beat a little faster as he brought his horse closer to her own. He leaned towards her and the mad thought that he might kiss her flashed across her mind, and yet she did not move.

Her hands had gone slack on the reins so when Countess suddenly moved forwards and kicked out her back legs at Hermes, she was not prepared. She fell forwards and clasped her round the neck, only just saving herself from a fall. She thought she heard a high-pitched, faint whistling and looked around in surprise and then stilled, her eyes wide.

Hermes had reared at the attack, avoiding the intended blow, but Harry had him under control in a matter of moments.

"What is it?" he said quickly when he saw Katherine's expression.

She pointed to something behind him. He glanced over his shoulder and then swiftly dismounted, striding over to a sheep that had collapsed onto its side. It twitched quite violently for a few moments and then went unnaturally still.

She saw him pull something from it and examine it closely.

Dismounting herself, she walked over to him.

"I heard a strange whistling sound," she began, but her words dried up as she saw what held his attention.

It was some sort of dart. It was slender, made of a light coloured wood and had a white feather on one end and a very sharp, glistening point on the other. It occurred to Katherine that it was not long enough to have reached any vital organ.

"My God!" he breathed, his eyes flashing angrily. "This could have hit you!"

"Or you," Katherine said quietly, her brain working rapidly. "Are you going to tell me it is a poacher again?"

Their glances again met and held, this time her heart hammering for a quite different, but just as alarming reason.

Amazed at how calm her voice sounded, she said, "A poisoned dart seems a little exotic for a Cornish poacher, don't you think? Not to mention the fact that it is the second time you have come close to being killed, my lord."

Lord Treleven was suddenly full of urgency. "Get back on your horse," he snapped. "We must return to the house, quickly. Whoever did this, may have more of them!"

They both turned and ran. Harry threw her

up into the saddle and then vaulted onto Hermes. Without speaking they raced back the way they had come, not slowing until they neared the stables.

"I must request that you say nothing of this to anyone," he finally said.

"But, surely—" she began, but he cut her off.

"To anyone! I will explain more to you when I can, you have my word. No one else is in any danger I am sure, and informing them of this will only inspire terror in my mother."

"You cannot go out again!" she said, startled. "They may still be out there."

"Do not alarm yourself, Miss Lockhart. I will not be so predictable in my movements this time and I hardly think there is someone lurking behind every bush."

"Do you know who is responsible?" she asked.

"Yes. There can be no doubt. But I hope that he will be dealt with by the end of today."

With that she had to be satisfied for he suddenly veered off, heading towards the home wood.

When she entered the house, she felt suddenly drained.

"You are back so soon?" Lady Treleven said,

surprised, just then coming into the hall with Belle.

"Why, you look quite pale," said Belle, concerned. "Are you ill?"

"Yes," Katherine murmured. "Yes, that is why I have returned. It is just a headache, I shall go and lie down for a while."

Belle came forward and took her arm. "Here, I will help you to your room."

When they were out of earshot of Lady Treleven, Belle murmured softly, "I hope Lord Treleven has not upset you in some way? He is a card, always jesting and sometimes quite outrageous but he means nothing by it, I assure you."

They had reached the door to her chamber and Katherine found herself quite unequal to the task of fielding any more questions. "Please, Belle, I cannot talk just now."

She closed her door softly behind her and leaned back against it, closing her eyes. What could it all mean? He had nearly kissed her and then he had nearly been murdered. Her head really was beginning to ache, it was filled with a jumble of images and tangled thoughts.

The wall of protection she had built around herself had crumbled to dust in the moment he had leant towards her, his eyes full of a gentle tenderness that had stopped her breath. She had never allowed even Mr Sharpe, a man who she thought she had been in love with, the liberty of a kiss, yet she had made no move to deny Lord Treleven. The pain of Mr Sharpe's betrayal and loss had been nothing to the stab of agony she had felt when she realised just how close Lord Treleven had come to death.

She stumbled to her bed and sank face down into her pillows, clutching them fiercely. Even if he had been about to kiss her, it meant nothing. He had given no other sign that he felt any great affection for her, and as Belle had pointed out, he was known for being outrageous. She must not refine too much upon it, the shared exhilaration of their ride and his clear admiration of her skill as a horsewoman had probably caused the moment of madness. He did, after all, have a history of behaving rashly.

She rolled onto her back and sighed long and deep. If only he came back safe, she thought she would forgive him anything, even nearly making a fool of her.

Harry's senses were heightened as he weaved an erratic course towards the Padstow road. But even though he remained watchful, part of his mind lingered on Miss Lockhart. What had he been thinking? He grimaced. He had not been thinking. When she had been flying along beside him, he had felt a kinship with her, the feeling deepening when she had shown her vulnerability by admitting to feeling lost. But the blush of pink in her cheeks and the green flecks dancing in her eyes had made him feel something else entirely. He had glimpsed the fire that lurked beneath her sobriety and self-possession. He wondered what had happened to her that she kept that side of herself locked away.

A wry grin curved his lips. Perhaps it was just as well for him that she did. The poise she had shown when presented with his bloodied arm had seemed to him unfeminine. He had not admired it then, but he was beginning to think he was a fool. She had displayed it again today, her cool head and clear thinking had understood the threat to them in an instant, but rather than falling into hysterics she had acted with alacrity, following his lead without a moment's hesitation.

He finally gained the road and saw a cloud of dust in the distance. The familiar sound of a troop of horses galloping reached his ears, and then a host of blue and gold uniforms met his eyes. Lord Hayward led the way. Harry raised his hand in acknowledgement to the troop, many of whom he knew, and fell in beside him.

"You got your permission, I see," he said.

Lord Hayward grinned. "After much outrage and complaint."

Harry chuckled. "I can imagine, Lord Humphrey has pompous down to a fine art!"

"Doesn't he just," agreed Lord Hayward.

"There has been a development," Harry said.

Lord Hayward showed no great surprise at his news.

"I wondered about the first incident," he admitted. "But now it seems clear he wanted you out of the way. It seems he had a change of heart once he had met you. Probably thought he could get you on side. It would be far more to his advantage than to have an unknown neighbour replace you."

Harry frowned. "All this for the chance of getting Henrietta?"

"Without your protection his offer might have gained more favour. But now it is also personal, I think. Mr Caldwell does not strike me as someone who likes to be crossed."

"He must be mad!"

Lord Hayward chuckled. "More than one man has been made mad by love."

"You're a mighty cool fish," Harry said.

"Usually," Lord Hayward said softly. "But I nearly killed a man with my bare hands, once, for love."

"Who?" he asked, intrigued.

Lord Hayward gave him his sleepy smile. "Ask your friend, Sir Philip, he knows all about it."

"You may be sure I will."

"I would not, however, compare myself to Caldwell. It was not done in cold blood but in the heat of the moment, and the provocation was great."

As they came to the mine, the workers stopped what they were doing and stood, mouths agape, as the cavalcade passed them. Mr Scorrier was soon seen scurrying towards them.

"What is the meaning of this?" he exclaimed.

Lord Hayward retrieved a rolled piece of parchment from his pocket, unfurled it, and waved it under the man's nose. "This is a document giving me the right to search this mine and seize anything that I might find that I feel should be handed over to His Majesty's government."

Mr Scorrier grabbed it and rapidly scanned its contents. "I would ask, sir, that you wait until Mr Caldwell can be sent for."

"I think not," replied Lord Hayward. "I will send two men down to investigate the adit that leads to the beach below, you will provide me with someone to guide them."

Grumbling and cursing under his breath, Mr Scorrier walked over to two men who sat on a pile of sacks, chewing on some bread. One of them hurried off, the other approached.

"You're wasting your time," Mr Scorrier assured them.

"That remains to be seen," said Lord Hayward.

Two of the dragoons dismounted and followed the man towards the mine entrance that was cut into the rock of the cliff.

"Get back to work, you layabouts!" Mr Scorrier shouted at the women and children who still stood, silently watching.

"He seemed very sure we would not find anything," Harry said. "Either he is a very convincing liar or he knows nothing about it."

"We can only act upon what we know," Lord Hayward said. "But I hope you are mistaken for we have truly shown our hand now. We will not get a second chance."

Mr Caldwell soon arrived, his colour high and his small eyes angry. He looked at Lord

Hayward in some amazement. "You! What have you to do with this outrage?"

"Good day, Mr Caldwell. I am merely over-seeing this investigation."

"What investigation?" he demanded.

"Calm yourself, sir," Lord Hayward said softly. "We are merely trying to discover what happened to the very valuable cargo that was aboard the East Indiaman that sank. If you have nothing to hide, you have nothing to fear."

A sly gleam brightened his eyes. "Oh, you will not find anything, of that you can be sure."

His eyes shifted to Harry. "And what right do you have to be here, sir?"

"Perhaps you should clarify that comment, Caldwell," he said softly. "Do you mean 'here' as in at the mine, or 'here' as in of this earth?"

Lord Hayward sent him a warning look.

"I wish you would not talk in riddles," Mr Caldwell said tersely. "I have no idea what you are referring to."

There was a murmuring as the two men who had been sent into the mine reappeared, their uniforms damp and grubby.

"Well," said Mr Caldwell. "And did you find anything?"

The soldier addressed Lord Hayward. "Nothing there, sir."

Mr Caldwell gave him a cold stare. "If you have quite finished disrupting my day, you may leave. You may be sure I shall be writing to both Lord Humphrey and the home secretary to complain."

They moved off slowly, disappointment writ clear on their faces. This time Harry and Lord Hayward brought up the rear.

"I was so sure," said Harry.

One of the dragoons who had conducted the search, rode back towards them. He pulled a piece of sacking out of his pocket and a small silver key.

"I didn't want to say anything in front of the mine owner, sir," he said quietly, "but something was down there, only it's been moved. There was also a wooden plank and a pile of rubble and rock next to the adit, sir, almost as if it had been blocked and recently cleared."

"Thank you, Roberts," he said, taking both items from his grasp.

He turned to Harry. "He must have got wind that the dragoons were about and taken the precaution of moving his booty." He looked at the little key. "We missed our chance, this is very little to go on."

"Let me see it," Harry said.

Lord Hayward went to drop it in his palm,

but Hermes sidled and it fell to the track. Harry quickly dismounted to retrieve it. He picked it up and glanced back towards the mine. A ragged little girl was running towards them.

"I do believe that is the little imp who you rewarded for trying to pick your pocket," he murmured.

"Sir, sir," she panted as she came up to them. "Ma said I should tell you, something happened last night. Everyone was told to finish their shift early 'n' that never happens. Likes his pound of flesh, she always says."

Lord Hayward smiled at her. "Thank your ma for me, will you."

"There's more," she said breathlessly, she was wheezing and suddenly she bent over, her emaciated body racked by a series of chesty coughs. "It's the dust," she explained. "Gets in the lungs, Ma says. Anyways, we were told to get home and stay there."

"And did you?" asked Lord Hayward.

She shook her head. "No, and I got a right clout for it."

"From Scorrier?" Harry asked, his face darkening.

"No," she grinned. "From Ma!"

"What did you see?" he asked gently.

Her eyes widened. "Ma told me I was making it up, but I weren't, honest."

"Making what up, child?" Lord Hayward said patiently.

"I saw old belly ache, that's Mr Scorrier, headed towards the mine, with four others. I think they were men, but they had a sort of dress on and a funny thing on their heads."

In a few swift moves Harry removed his cravat and wound it round his head into something resembling a turban.

The little girl laughed. "Yes, like that."

Harry reached into his pocket and retrieved his purse. He took her dirt-smeared hand in his and dropped some coins into it. "Tell your Ma to take you and the rest of your family and go home."

The little girl was speechless for a few moments. Her small fist closed around the coins. "Thank you, sir."

They watched as she turned and fled back down the track.

Lord Hayward gave him a lopsided smile. "That was very generous of you, Treleven, considering the information only confirms most of what we already know."

Harry grinned. "Don't give up yet, Hayward. The cargo is still here. Somewhere. He will have to move it sometime, and we must make sure we are there when he does."

"I cannot keep the king's dragoons here indefinitely," he said. "And then there is the business of keeping you alive in the interim."

Harry grinned, the light of battle in his eyes. "I'm a hard man to kill. Besides, I don't think all my nine lives are used up just yet, Hayward."

They had come to a crossroads.

"I'm for Helagon," Harry said.

"Give me a moment and I'll be with you."

After a brief exchange with one of the regiment, he returned.

Harry gave him a quizzical look. "Fancy yourself in the role of bodyguard, do you?"

Lord Hayward gave a lazy grin. "I hardly think even Caldwell would have the audacity to try and murder you twice in one day. Especially now, when he knows you're on to him."

CHAPTER 12

Katherine could not rest but nor did she feel up to facing the concerned enquiries she was sure to receive if she returned downstairs. She was pacing up and down restlessly when a timid knock fell upon her door. It opened a fraction and Mrs Abbott's head peeped around it.

"Oh good, you are awake. I did not wish to disturb you if you were sleeping, my dear."

"No, I tried but could not."

"So I can see," Mrs Abbott said gently. "I always find that a breath of fresh air helps a headache. Would you like to take a turn about the gardens with me?"

Katherine looked into the kind face of her relation and knew she could not lie through her teeth to her. She needed to remove herself for a few hours until she had regained her usual composure.

"Actually, I am feeling much better already. I think I will take the gig and go and visit Mrs Nance after all."

"Are you sure, my dear?" she said concerned. "You do not seem yourself."

"Yes, yes, I am quite sure," Katherine assured her.

"Well give me a moment, my dear, I must just fetch my bonnet and pelisse and I will be with you."

"There is no need, Mrs Abbott," she said quickly. "You have your flowers to plan, remember?"

"Oh, that can wait. I am your companion first and foremost, and it has occurred to me that I have been very lax of late, yes, very lax. It will not do. I shudder to think what Sir Richard would say at you gallivanting all over unaccompanied, I really do."

She was gone on those words, but returned not many minutes later with Belle and Henrietta in tow.

"We bumped into Mrs Abbott on our way back from the nursery," Belle smiled. "Edmund is happily trying to sink his boat in a tub of water, quite determined to find a way to make it stay on the bottom. As my presence appears to be superfluous to his requirements and we are quite exhausted from writing reams of invitations, we shall accompany you also."

"But then there will be no one to help Lady Treleven," Katherine pointed out.

"She has gone to call on Lady Humphrey," Henrietta said. "She decided to deliver her invitation in person. She has taken the carriage but perhaps we could take yours?"

Having finally run out of obstacles to throw in their path, Katherine capitulated.

She sat back and listened with only half an ear to their chatter.

"Although writing invitations is always dreary," Belle said, "I find it quite amusing to try to conjure up an image of an unknown person merely from their name. Sir Miles Hawkmoore is a case in point. I imagine him as a tall, regal sort of gentleman with a large, slightly curved nose and keen, observant eyes."

Henrietta giggled. "I am afraid you will be sadly disappointed when you make his acquaintance," she said. "He is short, stout, and wears spectacles."

"Really? How very vexing. What about Mr

Hogwood? He must surely be short, stocky and have little piggy eyes?"

Henrietta shook her head. "No, I am afraid you are again mistaken. He fits your first description much more accurately."

"How extraordinary. Are they of an age? Perhaps they somehow got mixed up when they were babes."

Katherine finally cracked a smile.

"I particularly enjoyed the appellation, Clutterbuck," chimed in Mrs Abbott. "It has quite a ring to it, don't you think? Although I think this person is harder to immediately envisage."

"Not at all," Belle disagreed. "He would be, I think, someone who dresses all by guess, nothing matching and his person would be decorated with an array of rings and fobs, but unfortunately none of his time pieces would be accurate, causing him always to be late."

She gave Henrietta an enquiring look.

"Mr Clutterbuck is nothing if not neat, I would go as far as to say he is austere in his appearance," Henrietta laughed.

"I wonder what you would have made of me, if you had only heard my name," Katherine said with a wry smile.

"Oh, but I think we have just established

that a name rarely defines the person, my dear," Mrs Abbott pointed out.

As they turned down the uneven lane to Helagon, the carriage lurched in its usual torturous fashion and Belle had to grab the strap to avoid being thrown against Mrs Abbott.

"Do not tell me you travelled all the way from Bath in this antiquated old thing?"

"Do not let my coachman hear you," Katherine smiled. "He assures me she's a fine old gal for a short journey!"

"He is mistaken," Belle said with some asperity.

As they neared Helagon they found their way blocked by a farmer's cart. He was drawn across the entrance to the drive. Katherine pushed down the window and peered out.

"Oh, his front wheel is damaged, we will have to walk the rest of the way."

"That will be no hardship," Belle said drily.

The unprecedented and quite alarming prospect of four very finely dressed ladies approaching him caused the farmer's eyes to widen and his ruddy cheeks began to glow as if lit from within.

"I'm mortified to have caused you such trouble, Miss Treleven, ladies," he said, touching his hat respectfully. "I knew it was loose, wouldn't have used the cart if it wasn't urgent."

"Whatever can have happened, Mr Treen?" said Henrietta gently.

"Oh, I'll not bother you with the details, miss, it's his lordship that I need to see."

"Well, my good man," Belle said, her eyes alight with curiosity, "you are about to have your wish granted."

Lord Treleven and Lord Hayward had just rounded the bend in the drive. When they saw the ladies clustered about the cart, they dismounted and walked to meet them. Harry threw Katherine an intent look and she shook her head slightly.

"In trouble, Treen?" Lord Treleven eyed the wheel that leant at a drunken angle.

"Never mind my cart, sir. You won't believe what 'as happened, it was like something out of the Bible."

Everyone stared at him in some amazement.

"Except o'course, my sheep aren't men and they never rebelled against anything in their short lives, apart from when they escaped the other day and I could hardly blame them for that."

"Are you feeling quite the thing, Mr Treen?" Henrietta said eventually.

"I knew you wouldn't believe it," Mr Treen declared.

"If you wish us to understand you, Treen, you must speak more plainly," Harry said brusquely.

"I think you will find," said Mrs Abbott, "that he is referring to the book of numbers, when the earth opened up and swallowed those who had rebelled against Moses."

"Didn't I just say so?" the farmer exclaimed.

"I have no idea," Harry admitted.

Lord Hayward exchanged a humorous look with his lady. "Are you trying to tell us that your sheep have been swallowed up by the earth, my good fellow?"

That good fellow, feeling much exasperated, looked at him as if her were a simpleton. "What else could I mean? An' I thought the gentry was meant to have lots o' learnin'."

Harry's lips twitched. "You must forgive my ignorance," he said, "but am I to take it that you need some help rescuing your sheep?"

"That I do, sir. I've had to lay off the lads as helped me, times being a little hard. I thought you might send me a man or two. I've got a rope and trusty Ben here," he said, patting his horse. "But it'll take someone with a head for heights to help me out of this, that's for sure. It's a miracle any of 'em are still alive. But I heard 'em, they was still bleatin' when I left."

Harry looked startled. "How deep is this pit they have fallen into?"

Mr Treen gave a harsh laugh. "Pit? It's no pit, Lord Treleven. More what you'd call an abyss."

Harry and Lord Hayward exchanged a meaningful stare.

"We will help you, Treen," Harry said, turning to mount his horse.

"But, sir, it's not fit—"

"Treen, stop blubbering and climb up on that coach."

Harry's tone was commanding, harsh even. The farmer looked at him as if he were a stranger, but nevertheless climbed up onto the roof of the coach.

He turned to the ladies. "We will return for you later."

"I don't think so," said Belle, completely unimpressed by his display of authority. "Come, ladies, I for one, want to witness for myself this act of God!"

As they moved towards the carriage, Harry raised an eyebrow at Lord Hayward. He seemed unruffled by his lady's proclamation and merely grinned.

"I wouldn't waste your breath," he advised. "Once Belle sniffs out a mystery there is no stopping her."

They fell in behind the coach. "I thought you had better control over your wife, Hayward."

His companion chuckled. "When you have one of your own, Treleven, you may pass judgement."

Katherine sank back into her seat in the coach and breathed long and low. Her heart had jumped at first sight of Lord Treleven, drumming in her ears as relief had swept through her. She had stood back and covertly observed him as he had tried to untangle Mr Treen's explanation of events. She had not missed his arrested expression when the depth of the pit had been explained, or the flame of excitement that had suddenly lit his eyes. She had been just as determined as Belle to see what had caused it but was grateful that her friend had taken the initiative, not at all sure she could have disregarded his wishes with such equanimity.

"I must admit I am very curious to see this abyss," laughed Belle. "I only hope Mr Treen is not prone to exaggeration for I will be most disappointed if we do not find something of biblical proportions."

They had drawn up beside a gate. Belle craned her neck and saw that her husband was unlatching it.

"Brace yourselves ladies," she said, dismayed. "For I fear we are about to cross a field."

They all immediately reached for the strap that hung by each door. They had not gone very far when Belle's usually rosy complexion, paled considerably.

"Belle?" said Katherine, "is something amiss?"

She received a frantic shake of the head by way of reply. They came to a stop not many moments later and Belle hastily opened the door, leaned out and was violently sick. Mrs Abbott searched in her reticule, retrieved her handkerchief and sprinkled it with the sal volatile she always kept there. As Belle straightened up, she offered it to her.

That grateful lady held it to her nose and breathed deeply. Almost immediately, her complexion improved.

"Thank you, Mrs Abbott," she said. "I will be quite alright now. That ghastly rocking made me feel just as I did when we were at sea. Say nothing to Hayward, I beg of you, he will only fuss."

Fortunately for her, he had not noticed. The

reason for this lack of consideration on his part was soon made abundantly clear. It appeared that Mr Treen was not prone to exaggeration after all, for there was indeed a yawning abyss in the middle of the field.

"I told you my sheep wouldn't go anywhere near that dip," said the farmer to Harry. "But when I came to move them to another pasture today, some had wandered in there, must have got used to it, I suppose. I thought nothing of it at first, then I heard a low rumble and they just disappeared."

The ladies joined them on the edge of the precipice. It must have been ten feet wide at least and who knew how deep, for they certainly could not see the bottom.

"Oh, Mr Treen," said Henrietta. "I think I have just heard one of your sheep."

They all listened for a moment, none of them really believing that anything could have survived such a fall, but sure enough, a faint bleat floated up to them.

Katherine's eyes widened as Harry stripped off his coat.

"Get that rope, Treen," he ordered.

"Sir!" The words were out before she could stop them. "Surely you are not going to risk your life for a sheep?"

He grinned and strode over to her, his eyes alight with excitement. "Do not concern yourself, ma'am," he said softly. "I know how to tie a knot that does not slip."

He took her hand and dropped a light kiss upon it. "There is more at stake than you know. Wish me good luck, ma'am, I am sorely in need of it."

"Good luck," she whispered, "and… be careful."

The rope was fetched. He tied one end of it to the coach and the other around his waist. They watched him confidently descend into the darkness below.

"Harry," Henrietta cried as he disappeared from view.

Mrs Abbott wrapped an arm about her. "Hush, child. Have faith. He did not survive Napoleon and years at sea to meet his maker in a muddy hole."

Time seemed to slow to a crawl as they all stood unmoving, their gazes solemn, as if they stood at the edge of an open grave. It seemed an eternity later when the rope that lay taut against the side of the cavernous opening twitched.

Lord Hayward stepped forwards and began to haul it in, hand over hand. Mr Treen took up position behind him and aided him in his efforts.

A bundle of white fluff slowly emerged, an out-
raged bleat preceding it.

Miraculously it had seemed to escape any
serious hurt, for the moment they had untied it,
it shook itself and gambolled off to join its fel-
lows who were huddled in the far corner of the
field.

Lord Hayward lowered the rope again. The
next time it jerked Katherine and Henrietta exchanged a small smile both sure they would see
Harry within a few moments. They searched the
darkness for a sign of his shining blond locks.
Instead two rough sacks appeared.

"What's all this?" said Mr Treen, bemused,
moving to open one.

"Do not touch it." Lord Hayward's voice
was stern and Mr Treen immediately ceased his
investigation.

Again and again the rope was lowered. Each
time it re-emerged with either a sack or box
attached.

Belle was sorely tempted to take a peek into
one and began to edge her way towards them.
Without so much as turning his head Lord Hayward addressed her, but in much gentler terms
than he had dissuaded Mr Treen.

"I think not, my dear."

With only the slightest hint of a pout, she rejoined the others. Eventually the blond locks that Henrietta and Katherine so earnestly wished to see, emerged from the dark. Harry was mud smeared but triumphant.

"We have him!" he grinned, shaking Lord Hayward's hand and laughing. "It seems there are no limits to that man's audacity after all, he has been mining under my own land! No wonder he either wanted me on side or out of the way! It seems however, that the workings were not well supported. They have collapsed and the tunnel is blocked. It is a shame your troop have gone on ahead, for we need to grab him before he realises."

Mr Treen looked bemused by this conversation. However he turned his mind to his most pressing concern.

"But my sheep, milord. Where are the rest of 'em?"

Harry sobered for an instant. "I am afraid they did not make it, Treen. The one I sent up had the good fortune to have a soft landing, it fell upon the others."

The farmer's face fell and Harry clapped him on the shoulder. "Do not fret, I will make sure you are compensated for every last one of them."

Mr Treen looked a little brighter.

"Help us get this lot onto the coach, will you? And not a word to a soul, you understand?"

"I can't say as I do, sir, but who would I tell anyways? The wife 'ud think I'd gone soft in the head if I told her this tale!"

"Good man!"

The ladies were bundled back into the carriage all their questions unanswered, whilst the sacks and boxes were tied to the roof.

Harry turned to the coachman who had remained stoically impassive throughout the proceedings, only offering advice on how best to secure the retrieved items on the roof.

"John, isn't it?" Harry said. "Take the ladies back to Elmdon and guard this carriage as if your life depends on it."

Coachman John nodded. "You may depend on me, sir." He tapped his coat pocket and winked. "I always carry a pistol, not that I've ever had to use it."

Satisfied, Harry turned to Lord Hayward. "Come, I will take you cross country, we can cut them off before they reach Padstow."

CHAPTER 13

L ady Treleven had returned when they reached Elmdon. They found her in the drawing room, her colour rather heightened.

"There you are," she said, "wherever have you been? I am full of news and have had no one to share it with."

"So are we, Mama," Henrietta said, sitting next to her. "We have had a very interesting morning."

"Oh have you?" Lady Treleven said. "You are very fortunate. Mine has been hideous. I have had to bear with Lady Humphrey crowing it over me with the most extraordinary tale." She gave Belle a hard stare. "Something about Lord Hayward conducting a search of the mine for the lost cargo of some ship or other, which of course, didn't exist. He has caused Lord Humphrey and myself considerable embarrassment, and made himself and Harry, who was also present at this outrageous event, a laughing stock. A very odd thing for him to do considering I thought him to be interested in acquiring a property."

Belle coloured. "I am sorry, ma'am. He does not always take me into his confidence about his business affairs. But I think you will find your embarrassment somewhat alleviated when you hear our news."

With much questioning back and forth, and many interruptions, they found they had the final piece of each other's puzzle.

"Ha! It is I who shall crow now!" Lady Treleven said, her indignation forgotten. "Or at least, I would, if I were a vulgar, encroaching creature, which I am glad to say, I am not."

"But why would Mr Caldwell need to steal anything?" Henrietta asked. "He is already so rich."

"Oh, how should I know, child? Greed I suppose. There is a reason greed is one of the seven deadly sins."

Katherine, who had kept very much in the background during this exchange, did not mention that he was also guilty of attempting another of these sins, one that, in her eyes at least, was far, far worse.

The ladies attempted to occupy themselves with the preparations for the ball. But even though they had not so many hours before been fully occupied with this endeavour, now topics such as how many candles would have to be ordered in, or the order of the dances, could no longer hold their interest for very long.

It was late in the afternoon before the gentlemen finally returned by which time they were agog with curiosity. Lord Treleven went to change his raiment before showing his face and so it fell to Lord Hayward to satisfy it.

"Hayward," Belle said, her face lighting up as she saw her husband. "Tell us everything, immediately."

Lord Hayward strode over to the fireplace, leant his arm on the mantelpiece and rested his booted foot on the fender. His face was a little grave.

"Is all well?" she enquired after a moment.

"We took Mr Caldwell unawares," he said after a moment. "He tried to deny all knowledge of course."

"Will you be able to prove his involvement?" asked Lady Treleven.

Lord Hayward glanced at her, his expression solemn.

"Without doubt, ma'am."

"To think of a neighbour of ours, having to stand trial."

"That will not be necessary," Lord Hayward said softly.

"Why ever not? Do not tell me that he can buy his way out of trouble?"

"It will not be necessary for Mr Caldwell to stand trial, ma'am, because he is no longer living."

The ladies gasped. After a moment Lord Hayward continued.

"He made the mistake of trying to throw the blame on Mr Scorrier who runs the mine for him. On perceiving the gravity of the crimes that were being laid at his door, that gentleman was easily persuaded to talk. Although this inevitably involved revealing his own part in the case, the crime of helping conceal the goods will carry a much lighter sentence than masterminding the whole."

"But how is Mr Caldwell dead?" Katherine asked. "Did he try to escape?"

"No, a couple of his servants made the attempt but we had the house surrounded."

"Was that to do with the other matter, sir?" Katherine asked quietly.

Belle's brows rose and she gave Katherine an enquiring look. "What other matter?"

Katherine bit her lip, unsure if she should have said anything, but she could not see what harm it could do now.

"Sabotaging an East Indiaman and stealing the cargo were not his only crimes," Lord Hayward explained.

He looked at Lady Treleven. "Apart from being almost certainly involved in fraudulent insurance claims, he tried, on two occasions to murder your son. The first attempt was put down to a poacher in the woods. The second attempt was made this morning, the method a poisoned dart, which fortunately missed its target."

Her hand flew to her breast, her eyes widening. She remained very much in control of her emotions however. "Then I am glad he is dead," she said flatly.

Belle's eyes were again on Katherine. "No wonder you were ill! But you said nothing of it."

"No, you did not," said Lady Treleven, clearly much put out. "Perhaps you did not think I would be interested in such a trifling event?"

Katherine flushed. "Lord Treleven had told me I must not. He did not want you to worry, ma'am. He assured me he hoped to have the matter resolved by the end of today."

Katherine was relieved when she turned her attention back to Lord Hayward. "How did he die? Did Harry—?"

"No, ma'am. Lord Treleven had the presence of mind to keep the dart, and an extensive search of the house revealed others as well as the blowpipe used. Once Caldwell realised that he would also be facing a murder charge and the hangman's noose, he took things into his own hands. He was seated at his desk in the library, and before we could stop him he had a drawer open and a pistol in his hand. He at first turned it upon Lord Treleven but then gave a queer sort of laugh and turned it upon himself. In short ma'am, he shot himself."

It was perhaps only to be expected that dinner that evening was a rather subdued affair.

"I will have to go up to town to give my report of events here." Lord Hayward dropped the words into one of the many silences.

"Oh, will you, my dear?" Belle said. "Will you be back for the ball?"

"I should think so," he smiled.

"You are, of course, welcome to stay for the ball," Lady Treleven said a trifle stiffly. "But was it really necessary to be my guests under false pretences?"

Her gaze encompassed both Belle and Lord Hayward.

"I really did not know what he was up to," Belle said.

"But you knew he was not looking for property, I think."

"Do not blame Lady Hayward, ma'am," Lord Hayward said. "It was not her fault. I was not at all sure of my ground and the fewer people who were aware of my interest in this affair, the better."

"Very well," she conceded. "As you have rid me of that man, I will forgive you."

"Thank you, ma'am."

He glanced at Harry. "Your evidence will also need to be heard so I suggest you accompany me."

"Oh surely that is not necessary," Lady Treleven protested. "The ball is barely ten days away! We can hardly hold a ball in your honour, Harry, if you are not present!"

"I have covered further distances in less time, I assure you, ma'am. Do not fret."

With that she had to be satisfied.

When the ladies had retired, Harry reached into his pocket and brought out the small silver key.

"I had almost forgotten this. Shall we see which box it fits?"

"If you wish," smiled Lord Hayward.

Their haul had been stored in Harry's study for safety until it could be collected in the morning. Most of the boxes were too large, but they finally found a small one, hidden in one of the sacks. It was square, quite plain, and made from Indian rosewood. The key fitted perfectly. Harry grinned and opened the lid. Inside, on a bed of red velvet lay a huge blue sapphire. It twinkled in the candlelight, its glitter reflected in his eyes.

"This alone must be worth a king's ransom," he breathed.

"Indeed it is, it is rumoured to be the largest one ever discovered."

Harry carefully closed and locked the box, returning it to where it was found.

"No wonder the king was so anxious it was found, he has ever been a collector."

"Have you considered what this might mean to you, Treleven?"

"To me?"

"Apart from the sapphire, it is a valuable cargo. There are other jewels, spices, tea, silk, and many other items. Items that you may claim salvage on as you recovered them."

"I had not thought of that," he said slowly.

"And I think you will find that I can ensure your claim does not take years to be settled."

They were away early, before breakfast. Katherine watched them for some time from her bedroom window, only turning away when they had finally faded from sight. She was glad, she told herself. She did not like her emotions to behave in the topsy-turvy fashion they had of late. By the time Lord Treleven returned the chances were she would have moved into Helagon and their friendship, if you could call it that, would become easier and more natural when they were not constantly thrown into each other's company.

The exciting events of the day before had precluded her visiting Mrs Nance and she mentioned her intention of rectifying this oversight at breakfast.

"I will come with you, if you like," said Henrietta.

That young lady seemed to be growing in confidence every day and although she did not much feel like company, Katherine did not have the heart to rebuff her.

"Yes, that is a very good idea, Henrietta,"

Lady Treleven approved. "I have asked Mrs Kemp to prepare some baskets of food and I would like you to take them to the vicarage, if you will. Harry mentioned that Mrs Creedley has been baking bread for the villagers and is quite at her wits' end but I am ashamed to say it had quite slipped my mind until he reminded me this morning."

At Helagon, they found the tiles had been replaced on the roof and work had started on the damaged ceilings. Fires had been lit in many of the rooms to dry them out and Katherine realised it would not be long before it was habitable again. She dashed a quick note off to her brother outlining the progress before heading for the kitchen.

Mrs Nance was more than happy to help with the preparations for the ball. She ran her eye over the list of items Mrs Kemp had suggested she help prepare. When she raised her head, it was Henrietta whom she addressed.

"If you don't mind, Miss Treleven, I used to be known for my lobster patties, might I add those to the list?"

Henrietta smiled at her. "Of course, Mrs Nance. We are very grateful for your help."

"You seem a little happier than before, Henrietta," Katherine said gently, as they approached Langarne.

"I am," Henrietta admitted. "I believe you were right, Miss—"

Katherine raised a brow.

"Katherine," she amended. "Both you and Belle have raised my spirits. What happened no longer seems quite so terrible. And I believe some of your confidence may be rubbing off on me!"

"I will remind you of that comment on the night of the ball," she smiled.

"You may need to," Henrietta admitted ruefully. "As soon as a gentlemen starts to flatter me, I feel most uncomfortable and can find nothing to say."

"Do you know, I have been known to suffer from the same malady myself?"

"You are just trying to make me feel better," Henrietta said.

"Not at all, let us practise. We shall take it in turns to be the gentleman. Who shall go first?"

Henrietta laughed. "I shall."

She cleared her throat and then said in a gruff voice. "Your lips look sweeter than cherries, ma'am."

Katherine choked. "Do not tell me someone actually said that to you?"

Henrietta giggled and nodded. "But how would you reply?"

"Like all things tried out of season, they oftentimes prove sour, sir."

"Oh, I would never think of saying anything like that."

"Then you must practise," Katherine said. "If that is the flavour of your compliments, try this one: "Your complexion is as fresh as morning dew.""

Henrietta's brow furrowed as she sought a reply. Then she grinned. "But will fade as quickly when too bright a light is shone upon it."

"Very good," Katherine smiled.

"Oh, I have one! You are as modest as a dove, my lady."

Katherine quirked a questioning brow.

"Oh yes," Henrietta assured her. "I have had that said to me also."

Katherine raised her chin in a haughty manner. "And can fly away from danger just as fast."

They had reached the vicarage. "Just treat it all as a game," she smiled. "And enjoy it, it is what I intend to do."

They found Mrs Creedley in a much improved humour.

"My mother has sent some baskets of food to hand out," Henrietta said.

"That's very kind of her." Mrs Creedley took them from her. "But let's hope there won't be any need for 'em much longer. Mr Gulworthy is just writing his sermon but I will fetch him directly."

They had not long to wait as the vicar soon came in, his faded blue eyes looking quite distracted.

"Ladies," he smiled.

"I apologise if we have interrupted your sermon," said Henrietta.

"Nonsense, nonsense, the distraction is welcome."

"I suppose you must have a funeral to prepare," said Katherine quietly.

Mr Gulworthy brushed his hand across his balding pate and shifted a little uneasily in his chair.

"Well that all depends, yes, it all depends."

"On what, sir?" asked Henrietta.

"Whether or not he is deemed to have been in his right mind."

The door opened on his words and Doctor Fisher came into the room.

"Jennings is much improved—" He paused when he saw they had visitors. "Miss Treleven, Miss Lockhart."

Katherine noted that a faint pink tinge had crept into Henrietta's cheeks.

"Well that is capital news. Well done, my boy," the vicar said, stepping forwards to shake his hand. He turned to the ladies. "Jennings is the poor miner who lost his leg."

Katherine looked interested. "It is indeed a feather in your cap, sir, if he has not only survived the procedure but is recovering also."

"Well it was touch and go to begin with," the doctor admitted. His eyes rested for a moment on Henrietta. "But I am sure Miss Treleven cannot wish to hear of such things."

"You are mistaken, sir," she said raising her eyes to his. "I am happy to hear of your success."

"Of course you are," the vicar smiled. "We shall drink a toast to Mr Jennings. A small glass of wine will do us no harm."

They had all just lifted their glasses to their lips when Mrs Creedley bustled in with the tea tray. She put it down none too gently on a side table and put her hands on her hips.

"I'm surprised at you, Mr Gulworthy, serving the ladies wine and at such an hour. Does not the Bible say it bites like a snake and poisons like a viper?"

"Now, now, Mrs Creedley, did not Jesus himself turn water into wine?"

Ignoring this unanswerable conundrum, she poured out a cup of tea and passed it to Henrietta, firmly removing the glass from her fingers.

"Here you are miss, I think you will enjoy this far more than that muck."

The work at Helagon was completed a few days before the ball but Lady Treleven persuaded Katherine to delay her departure until after it.

"I am sure we will find there are a thousand things that need to be done at the last moment," she assured her. "Besides, Henrietta is much improved since your arrival, Miss Lockhart, but it may well be that she becomes a little nervous on the evening of the ball. She will benefit from having her friends around her."

When her son had not yet arrived home the evening before the event, she grew very twittery.

"I knew it," she said irritably at dinner that evening. "He will not make it back in time. How I will explain his absence I do not know."

"Oh, do not be despondent, ma'am," Belle said confidently. "I am sure Hayward will have him back in time."

"Well, I hope he does. If he hadn't dragged Harry into this in the first place, we wouldn't be in this predicament."

"No, ma'am," Belle said meekly.

Lady Treleven threw her a suspicious look and then a reluctant grin twitched at the corners of her lips. "Belle Hayward, you are many things but meek isn't one of them. However, I apologise for being such a crosspatch. We are none of us able to control the actions of our menfolk after all."

They arrived soon after the tea tray had been brought into the drawing room. Belle flew out of her chair to greet her husband, who un-caring of his audience, caught her neatly about the waist and dropped a brief kiss on her up-turned cheek.

"Forgive us for coming in in all our dirt," smiled Harry.

Katherine noticed that he was looking tired but happy. She was aware her heart was beating a little faster and gave herself a little inward shake. She might not be able to help being a little in love with him but she would not add to the ranks of probably countless women, who had shown it before her.

"Never mind your dirt," said Lady Treleven.

"I am just happy that you are home in time for the ball."

Harry kissed her hand. "Forgive me, Mother. I did not wish to worry you."

Lady Treleven sat a little straighter in her chair. "No, about a great many things it would appear." Her tone was astringent. "I wish to inform you, Harry, that I am not made of china, and will not break every time an ill wind blows. From now on, you—" she paused and her gaze swept over the other occupants of the room, "and everyone else will keep me fully informed of any and all events occurring that pertain to you, Henrietta or Elmdon. Do I make myself clear?"

His face remained grave but Katherine did not miss the twinkle that lurked in his eyes.

"Then I had better inform you, ma'am, that we will very soon own Thornbury House and be the major shareholder in the mine."

Lady Treleven blinked in astonishment. "But how can that be?"

"Although Mr Caldwell met his end here, it was felt that the inquest should be held in London as he was best known there and his crimes mostly affected various people who had interests there," Lord Hayward explained. "The king himself took an interest in the hearing."

"And what was the outcome of this inquest?" Lady Treleven asked.

"A verdict of felo-de-se was recorded, ma'am. It is more usual in these cases for a verdict of non compos mentis to be given but as Mr Caldwell does not seem to have any living relatives, and had severely depleted his resources with the acquisition and very expensive renovation of Thornbury House, it was deemed fair. His assets are now confiscated by the Crown and will be used to offset the cost of the ship that was lost among other things."

Lady Treleven was now receiving all the information she could wish for but seemed quite overwhelmed by it all.

"I am owed salvage on the items recovered," Harry explained. "As well as compensation for the unlawful intrusion into my land, not to mention mineral rights on the ore removed. The amount due will be offset against the property and the mine so, in effect, ma'am, we have acquired both for very little."

"I see," she said, a small frown between her eyes. "But, Harry, what do we want with them?"

Harry looked a little rueful. "A fair question, ma'am, and one I would have asked myself not so long ago. Whether we like it or not, however, mining is the blood of this county. I did not aspire to be a mine owner but it has been borne upon me that it is the only way we can ensure the continued wellbeing of our people, and ensure their working conditions are as safe as possible. As for the house, at least we can have some say in who becomes our neighbour."

"Very true," she said brightening. She cast a glance at her daughter. "I have asked the vicar and Doctor Fisher to dine with us tomorrow."

She smiled as she saw the delicate flush that stole into Henrietta's cheeks.

"You must hope that he remains here," Katherine said. "For no matter how safe you make the mine, there are likely to be accidents. I was very impressed that he was able to save a miner's life even though he lost his leg."

"Managed it, did he?" Harry lips twisted into a lopsided grin. "How very disappointed you must have been not to have witnessed the procedure."

Katherine grimaced. "I do not think I would have had the fortitude to withstand such a sight."

"I think you underestimate yourself, ma'am," he said gently. "You have more fortitude than any other female of my acquaintance. A circumstance I have every reason to be thankful for."

Katherine saw admiration in his eyes and became quite tongue-tied. Fortunately Lady Treleven was not so incapacitated.

"Is there anyone in particular you would like to invite for dinner, Harry?" she enquired.

"We have enough geese to feed a small army," she added drily.

Harry raised an amused brow. "How so?"

"I have not been able to consult with Mrs Kemp any time in the last few days, without one or other of your tenants appearing at the kitchen door with a goose, hoping the offering would soften the blow that they need a little longer to pay their rent."

"Then it is fortunate that I am very partial to goose," he laughed.

CHAPTER 14

At last everything was ready. Torches and lanterns had been placed at intervals along the drive, the long unused ballroom gleamed by the light of hundreds of candles and the floor had been polished to a bright sheen.

Henrietta stood with her mother looking radiant and quite beautiful in her simple white gown, her golden locks crowned by a wreath of pomegranate blossoms. Her brother lounged beside her, his dark coat and silk breeches relieved by the white waistcoat and stockings he wore. Indeed, Katherine reflected, they made a startlingly beautiful picture.

As she passed Henrietta, she leaned forwards and whispered in her ear, "I do not think any compliment you receive tonight could be called exaggerated, but remember, view it is a game and enjoy it."

"I shall," she assured her.

As she dropped a light curtsey to Harry he caught her hand and raised it to his lips, causing it to tremble slightly in his grasp. His eyes surveyed her pale pink gown and then lingered on her cheek a moment.

"You look charming, Miss Lockhart," he smiled. "Like a delicate rose."

Determined to follow her own advice she ignored the fluttering of her heart and raised an arch brow. "Beware, sir, for there never was a rose without a thorn."

"Hornet," he murmured, grinning.

Mrs Abbott was behind her and he also bowed deeply over her hand.

"I do hope you will save me a dance, my good lady," he said.

Katherine smiled, it was quite clear from the long train of her gown that Mrs Abbott had no intention of dancing but she appreciated the kindness he had shown her companion. She had come to realise he was kind, in his own careless fashion. He had also shown great concern and care for both his family and his tenants. In short, whatever his past, he was a good man. One she had been too quick to judge.

Even though she had moved further into the room, she heard the high-pitched titter of Miss Humphrey. Looking over her shoulder she saw that young lady playfully rap her fan against Lord Treleven's arm. She sighed. It was a timely reminder that all the qualities she had just acknowledged in him did not alter the fact that he was a flirt, and not to be taken at all seriously as far as affairs of the heart were concerned.

"Oh, the orchestra is about to play, I think," Mrs Abbott said. "And I have not forgotten your forfeit, my dear."

Katherine smiled down into the suddenly mischievous eyes of her companion. "I had forgotten it," she admitted. "Come, I am ready, what is it to be?"

"You must dance every dance you are solicited for this evening, that is all."

"You have wasted your forfeit then," she said. "For that was already my intention."

At that very moment, a rather portly gentleman with twinkling brown eyes and a pair of small spectacles perched on his rather snub nose, bowed before her.

"Sir Miles Hawkmoore," he smiled. "Forgive me introducing myself but I think we can dispense with the usual formalities at a private ball. May I have the honour of this dance, ma'am?"

Katherine threw an amused glance at Mrs Abbott and smiled so widely at him that he flushed.

As she took up her place in the set forming she noticed Doctor Fisher, who looked quite splendid this evening, lead Henrietta onto the floor. Belle was not far behind. She was being remarkably unfashionable and dancing the first with her husband. She radiated happiness and love. They had been married for some years now but still only had eyes for each other. She sighed and was aware of a slight twinge of envy. How wonderful it must be to know you were truly loved and have the unshakeable faith in your partner that Belle frequently displayed.

She very nearly stumbled as her partner turned her, and shook off the thought. She would make some sort of useful life here and be content with her lot. And she would begin by thoroughly enjoying this evening.

It did not prove too difficult a task, for finding herself to have the merit of novelty amongst a set of people who had known each other all their lives, she found herself with a succession of partners, all eager to please. Witnessing Henrietta blossom enhanced her pleasure further. On more than one occasion she observed her cause her partner to laugh and could only assume she was enjoying the game of light flirtation.

During a lull between dances, Belle found her. "Is it not wonderful?" she smiled, pointing with her fan to where Henrietta stood surrounded by admirers, holding court. "I would not have thought it possible that the shy wallflower I knew would transform herself into the incomparable of the ball."

"It is as it should be," Katherine said. "For she outshines every other young lady present."

"Indeed," agreed Belle. "I can see one lady in particular who seems most put out."

Katherine followed her gaze and saw Miss Humphrey on the edge of Henrietta's group of admirers. Her shrill laugh rent the air causing them both to wince.

"If she bats her eyelashes or waves her fan any harder, the young man she is trying to engage will think she is having a fit," Belle said drily.

As they watched, Lord Treleven paused near the group and said something in Doctor Fisher's ear before sauntering in their direction. Miss Humphrey, catching sight of him, snapped shut her fan and hurried after him, leaving the young man she had so recently been attempting to be-guile with her wiles, staring after her, his mouth agape.

Lord Treleven had nearly reached them when she caught up with him and snatched at his arm.

"There you are, Lord Treleven, where have you been hiding?" she tittered a trifle breath-lessly, unfurling her trusty fan once more and waving it in front of her face. "It is dreadfully hot in here, is it not? I am sure you would know of a quiet spot where a lady could cool herself."

Belle's brow rose. "The little minx!"

The music struck up and the young lady glanced hopefully up at her quarry.

Harry bowed and she flushed with excite-ment. "Might I suggest you sit this one out, Miss Humphrey, as you are so warm? I believe I am promised to Miss Lockhart for this dance."

Turning neatly on his heel he took a step in her direction, bowing and offering her his arm. Following strictly the terms of her forfeit, she placed her hand on it lightly and allowed herself to be led onto the floor.

"That poor child," she murmured re-provingly.

His eyes laughed down at her causing her heart to miss a beat. "She will not be a child much longer if she carries on in her present fashion."

"Perhaps she was a little forward," she conceded.

"There is no perhaps about it," he said with some asperity. "If she tries that with the wrong man she will find herself in the suds. She is completely without the dignity and modesty that mark your manners, ma'am."

The dance was a cotillion and left them little opportunity for further private conversation. Katherine was grateful, for every time they came together and she was forced to look into his eyes, she found herself without a single sensible thought in her head. She certainly would not have been able to parry his compliments with the wit necessary to both keep him firmly in his place and conceal how deeply they affected her.

He bowed deeply before her as it came to an end. "You dance delightfully," he murmured. "I hope to claim another before the night is out."

She offered only a small smile by way of a reply.

She found Mrs Abbott enjoying a conversation with Mr Gulworthy.

"We are planning a rose garden for Helagon," she smiled. "Are you enjoying yourself, my dear?"

"Yes," she smiled. "I hope you are satisfied? I have followed the terms of our bargain to the letter and have danced every dance."

"Ah, but the evening is not yet over, my dear," she said softly. "And if I am not much mistaken you are about to be claimed again."

Katherine turned her head to see who might be approaching. And froze. The blood leached from her face and she had to fight the urge to flee the room.

A gentleman dressed in full regimentals stood before her. He had a handsome countenance and a fine figure.

"Miss Lockhart." He bowed, displaying an elegant leg. "Would you do me the honour of granting me the next dance?"

The denial that she longed to utter refused to push past the lump that had formed in her throat.

"Off you go, dear," Mrs Abbott gently encouraged her.

Unwilling to cause a scene, she capitulated. She had to stop a groan as the opening bars of what was unmistakeably a waltz drifted through the air. She could have sworn the next dance was meant to be a quadrille. She felt every fibre of her being stiffen as her partner placed an arm around her neat waist and took her hand in his.

They had danced many times before but she felt as if he were a stranger. The man she had thought she had known had been an imposter after all. She made no attempt to break the awkward silence that hung between them. She had nothing to say to him.

"I had not thought to find you here, ma'am," he finally said.

She merely raised an eyebrow.

"But I am glad," he continued. "I have often wondered what had become of you."

"I believe I am the spinster you had expected me to become, Mr Sharpe," she said through gritted teeth.

He had at least the grace to look uncomfortable. "You do not look like a spinster," he said softly, "but a beautiful young lady."

Her eyes flashed. "You cannot expect me to believe a word you say to me, surely?"

"I meant it, nonetheless," he said gently.

"What are you doing here?"

"My regiment has been stationed near here in support of an investigation into a missing ship. Most have returned to town but some of us remain whilst a few loose ends are tied up."

Everything fell into place. Lord Hayward had mentioned dragoons, but he had not said which regiment. It had not crossed her mind that it might be Mr Sharpe's.

"I hope they will be tied up soon, then," she said coolly.

He flinched a little at her words. "Come, Miss Lockhart. Cannot we at least part friends?"

She looked at him in some amazement. "An honest enemy is better than a false friend, sir."

She breathed a sigh of relief as the dance came to an end. Noticing Miss Humphrey hovering in the vicinity, clearly hopeful of an introduction, and overtaken by a sort of malicious humour quite foreign to her nature, she promptly obliged her.

Her enjoyment of the evening was at an end but she would not repay Lady Treleven's kindness or invite unwanted speculation or comment by retiring early, however much she might wish to do so. Feeling herself quite incapable of exchanging polite pleasantries with anyone just yet, she made her way to the retiring room hoping for a few quiet moments to collect her thoughts.

She was not to have them. Barely had she sunk into a chair before the door opened and Belle tripped into the room. To her great mortification it took just one sympathetic glance from her friend before she found her eyes suddenly swimming in tears.

"I thought something was amiss," Belle said gently, seating herself beside her and taking her hand, cradling it on her lap. "I know you are probably wishing me at Jericho but I think you will feel better if you share your troubles."

When Katherine remained silent, she rubbed her thumb gently over the back of her hand and said, "Shall I begin? I think you had met the gentlemen you have just danced with somewhere before. Judging by your stiff posture and forbidding countenance throughout the encounter, he has perhaps injured you in some way."

Katherine gave a rather grim smile. "Lord Hayward is sadly mistaken not to take you into his confidence when he carries out his business, Belle. Your extraordinary prescience would prove to be invaluable, I am sure."

"I have often told him so," Belle said lightly. "But every man likes to think he is master of his own affairs after all."

Katherine gave a rather hard little laugh. "Some like to imagine themselves master of everyone else's affairs also."

"Well, you will have to tell me it all now, for I am quite intrigued. Come, unburden yourself, you will feel better for it, I am sure."

Belle allowed Katherine to tell her halting

tale without interruption. When she had finished she said, "I think you will find that he is not alone in his opinions, my dear. But to treat you in such a way was quite unnecessary, callous even, and to practise such a deception on a young impressionable girl, unforgiveable. I am very pleased you introduced him to Miss Humphrey, I am sure they deserve each other."

Katherine gave a watery chuckle.

"There, that is much better," approved Belle.

"Thank you," Katherine said. "It is quite ridiculous that I was so overcome. I now realise I was not even in love with him, after all. But he took me by surprise and all the old feelings of humiliation and anger seemed very fresh again. But I am better now."

During his days away, Harry had found Miss Lockhart filling his thoughts with increasing frequency. Images of her smiling face as she steered his boat or rode Countess beside him had come unbidden as he had tried to sleep. He had found himself looking forward to coming home, knowing she would be there. Her quick tongue, swift intelligence and dignified demeanour had become increasingly appealing to him. She might have a managing disposition but she was also calm when other ladies he had known would have had hysterics. He would, he realised, like to know her better.

He strode purposefully over to the recess in the far corner of the room that housed the orchestra.

"Play a waltz next, will you?"

He turned and scanned the room. He saw his quarry in conversation with Mrs Abbott and a wolfish grin lightened his countenance.

"Ah, there you are, Treleven. I've been meaning to have a word with you. Like you to fill me in on the details of the inquest, if you would. Should have taken place down here by rights, but then everything about this business has been highly irregular."

Harry frowned down at Lord Humphrey. "Now is hardly the time, sir. I will call on you tomorrow."

He had taken no more than a couple of strides towards Miss Lockhart when he saw Hugh Sharpe was before him. Damn Humphrey, that pompous old windbag had made him miss his chance. Deciding if he could not dance with Miss Lockhart he would enjoy watching her instead, he retreated to the edge of the ballroom. Leaning his shoulder against the wall, he folded his arms and prepared to watch her glide gracefully around the room.

His brows rose in surprise and he straightened his posture before he had watched her for many moments. He had witnessed first hand her grace and elegance when she had danced with him earlier, but now, although her feet made all the correct steps, her posture was rigid where it should have been fluid and her face was like a mask, cold and pale.

He did not know Hugh Sharpe all that well, he had been part of what his friends had called the king's sect, a group of soldiers who were extremely patriotic but a little too serious and arrogant for his tastes. He could not imagine what he had said to disturb Miss Lockhart, but upset her he assuredly had.

Damping down the desire to march over there and wrench her out of his arms, thus causing a scandal he was sure she would deplore, he gritted his teeth and mustered what patience he could. He waited only for her to hurry off the dance floor in the direction of the retiring room before he made his move. Striding purposefully up to his guest and completely ignoring Miss Humphrey, with whom he was in conversation, he said peremptorily, "Sharpe, in my study, now."

Not waiting for a reply he turned on his heel and strode out of the ballroom. Mr Sharpe followed in his wake, a bemused look upon his face, leaving Miss Humphrey staring after them, her pout firmly in place.

Barely had he shut the door behind them before he said deceptively gently, "I did not invite you here, Sharpe, to upset my guests. You will explain to me precisely and without prevarication, what you said to cause Miss Lockhart distress."

"It was not my intention to—" he began.

"Did I not say precisely and without prevarication?"

This time the menace behind the words was unmistakeable. Mr Sharpe's colour heightened and resentment shone from his narrowed eyes.

"I do not believe I need to explain my actions to you, Treleven."

Harry reacted with lightning speed, his hands were around Sharpe's throat before he was fully aware of his own intentions. He pushed him up against the door and almost lifted the man off his feet. "If you wish to live very much longer, there is every need."

Mr Sharpe had gone very red in the face, his hands clawing ineffectually at Harry's arms.

"All right," he finally choked out.

Harry released him and he staggered to a chair, clutching his throat.

Harry strolled over to his desk and poured out a measure of brandy. He handed it to Mr Sharpe who swallowed it gratefully.

"I was unaware of your interest in that direction," he finally said, his voice hoarse. "Much can be forgiven a man who is in love."

Harry perched on the edge of his desk, his gaze hard.

"I am still waiting."

"Just remember, Treleven, that what I am about to relate to you happened years ago."

Harry listened with increasing disgust to his tale. No wonder Miss Lockhart had developed brittle armour to protect herself. Her confidence in her worth must have been decimated by this man's actions.

"What was wrong with you, man?" he snapped. "That you felt the need to humiliate a defenceless woman?"

Mr Sharpe sat a little straighter in his chair. "It is our job to uphold the values of our country, Treleven. We protect the natural order. There are many factions who could threaten it. Give a woman too much freedom and who knows where it will end? I have seen some who already try to rule their husbands, give them enough scope and they will think they can rule the country as well. You do not wait for a snake to strike but cut off its head before it gets the chance."

Harry saw the fanatical light in his eyes and did not waste his breath arguing with him.

"Get out of my house, Sharpe," he said walking to the door and holding it open. "You are the worst sort of fool."

"Oh, and what sort is that?" Mr Sharpe asked as he got to his feet.

"I saw you trying to engage Miss Lockhart, Sharpe. I cannot imagine that you have spent so much time in her company without realising what a fine creature she is. I think you held a torch for her. I think you may still. That makes you the sort of fool who cuts off his nose to spite his face."

Harry closed the door behind him and went again to the brandy decanter. He filled a glass and sat in his favourite wingback chair, swirling the liquid gently around the bulbous vessel, his gaze distracted. Although he wished to get to know Miss Lockhart better, Mr Sharpe's revelations had given him pause for thought. He could not in all good conscience trifle with Miss Lockhart's affections unless he was deadly serious in his intent. He had no desire to cause her pain.

On the contrary, he was conscious of a desire to protect her, even if it was from himself.

It was perhaps not surprising that Katherine should have noted the absence of the two gentlemen who had affected her heart most deeply when she returned to the ballroom. But any measure of relief she might have felt was to be short lived.

Miss Humphrey, who had made it quite clear to all her friends and acquaintances, that it was she they had to thank for the much anticipated Michaelmas ball, (and may even have gone as far as hinting that Lord Treleven's acquiescence to the scheme was in no small part due to the flattering interest he showed in her happiness), found herself disappointed in her expectations of the evening.

That the two most dashing gentlemen present had both danced with Miss Lockhart, who was clearly on the shelf, in preference to herself was mortifying to one who had long considered herself to be the acknowledged beauty of the neighbourhood. That this was largely due to the absence of Henrietta at most social events had never worried her overmuch, for even when she did appear she was so shy and tongue-tied that most young gentlemen preferred her own more vivacious style. That she had been forced into the background by the quite startling change in Miss Treleven that had resulted in her stealing her usual crowd of admirers, completed her humiliation.

She had watched enviously as various ladies were twirled around the room during the waltz, a dance that her mother thought scandalous and had strictly forbidden her to partake in. Her gaze had been inevitably drawn to the dashing Mr Sharpe. Although sensitivity to the feelings of others was not her forte, even she had noticed the constraint that had seemed to exist between that gentleman and Miss Lockhart, and she had quite correctly assumed that they had some sort of past connection that had not turned out well. As she saw Miss Lockhart return to the ball-room, she saw an opportunity to offer her low spirits some small measure of relief.

"There you are, Miss Lockhart," she said, hurrying up to her. "I have been so looking forward to furthering our acquaintance."

Katherine's mobile brows arched in surprise. "Have you?"

Undeterred by this rather dampening response, she rushed on. "Why of course, we so

seldom have outsiders move to the neighbourhood."

She took Katherine's arm. "Come, walk with
me a little."

Belle sent her a laughing look and went in
search of her husband.

"I must thank you for introducing me to Mr
Sharpe, a most interesting gentleman."

"I am glad you found him so," Katherine
murmured.

"Oh yes, indeed I did. And I am glad that
both he and Lord Treleven have shown you such
a flattering amount of attention. It is always
more comfortable is it not, to be made welcome
when one is in new surroundings?"

"Indeed."

"And of course they are both firm friends,
they served together at Waterloo, did you know?
I thought it very kind of them to choose to dis-
tinguish a more, shall we say, mature lady, when
there are so many others desirous of a partner.
Although I wouldn't set too much store by it, if I
were you."

"I set no store by it at all, I assure you," she
said coolly.

"I am so relieved. You seem such a dignified
lady but gentlemen can be so naughty sometimes, can't they? I think they cooked up some

sort of joke between them, for I had only been talking to Mr Sharpe for a short while when Lord Treleven whisked him off to his study. They were laughing about something or other as they left, indeed they seemed most amused. I thought I heard them mention your name although I may well have been mistaken."

Miss Humphrey had been working her malice in the dark, not sure if anything she said would hit home. But it appeared she had struck lucky for her companion had turned quite pale.

"Oh, do not take it to heart, ma'am. I would not wish to cause you any distress and if they have been having a little joke, if not a wager, at your expense, I am sure they mean no harm. But I felt it only right that I put you a little on your guard."

Katherine gently disengaged her arm. "Thank you for your consideration, Miss Humphrey, but it was unnecessary I assure you. I really have very little interest in either gentleman."

Miss Humphrey smiled, baring her little yellow teeth. "Well that is all right, then, now if you will excuse me I must just check on Mama."

Although it was clear to Katherine that Miss Humphrey's words were motivated by jealousy, their poison nevertheless seeped through her armour. Could it be that Lord Treleven knew of what had passed between her and Mr Sharpe? Had he invited him here knowing of their history? Had they both been laughing at her? Mr Sharpe had assured her that he had not expected to find her here. But then he had already proved himself a consummate liar. It was harder for her to believe that Lord Treleven would play so cruel a trick; indeed her heart assured her that he would not. But then her heart had been wrong before.

Katherine was glad that the ball was nearing its end and she could slip away to her room without occasioning any comment. It was a long time before she fell asleep however, her mind sifting through Miss Humphrey's words trying to separate the fact from the fiction.

CHAPTER 15

Katherine awoke to a grey overcast sky, her eyes as heavy as the rainclouds outside her window. Her musings of the night before had not led her to any firm conclusions and she decided she would not give the matter any further thought. Even if Miss Humphrey's assumptions were correct they did not in any material way affect her future. She may have developed a foolish tendre for Lord Treleven, but she had never for a moment allowed herself to hope that the feeling might be returned and the gentleman in question had certainly never given her any cause to think so.

"Are we packed, Ayles?" she asked, lethargically dragging the brush through her hair.

"Yes, ma'am." She took the brush from

Katherine's hand. "Here, let me, you'll be here all day at that rate."

She did not much feel like going down to breakfast but as she needed to take her leave of the Trelevens, it was unavoidable.

"Ah, there you are," smiled Lady Treleven, "we had almost given you up! Belle has not made it down, but I should think she needs to rest a little this morning."

"I'm afraid I slept in a little late," Katherine smiled.

"And no wonder, after all the excitement of the ball. It was a great success, I think."

"Yes, yes, it was," Katherine said, resisting the urge to look at Lord Treleven.

"There can be no doubt of it," agreed Mrs Abbott. "I have rarely enjoyed myself more."

"You left a little early, ma'am," Harry said. "I trust you did not feel unwell?"

Katherine's eyes lifted and she noticed he looked a little distant. "No, sir, not at all. But I am unused to dancing until dawn these days."

She turned to Henrietta and smiled. "You seemed to be enjoying yourself. You certainly proved to be a hit!"

Henrietta's eyes twinkled. "I did enjoy it. I played our little game and think I did you proud!"

"Game?" Lady Treleven said. "What game was this?"

"Miss Lockhart helped me learn how to reply to a gentleman's compliments. They had always embarrassed me before, but she taught me to turn it all into a game and how to answer the more silly ones."

Lady Treleven gave Katherine a look of approval. "Give me an example of this game, Henrietta."

"Mr Hogwood informed me that I was a bright shining star."

"Really?" said Lady Treleven. "He has always struck me as very dignified, a little too puffed up in his own conceit even. I do hope you gave him a set-down for his impertinence?"

Henrietta assumed a haughty, bored look and said in a languid voice, "I do hope not, sir, for I do not intend to fade with the dawn."

Harry choked on his coffee.

Lady Treleven looked quite amazed. "Henrietta! Although I am glad you found a way to enjoy your evening, I do hope you will not put on those airs and graces as a matter of course!"

"No, Mama, it was just a game."

"Did Doctor Fisher pay you silly compliments?" she asked after a moment.

Henrietta laughed. "He is far too much a

gentleman and has enough sensible conversation that he does not need to resort to such tactics, thank heavens."

"Oh, I see," her mother said. "And do you enjoy sensible conversation?"

"It is the only kind I enjoy," her daughter informed her.

"Miss Lockhart's influence again makes itself felt," Harry murmured.

The rattle of rain against the windows caught his attention.

"Are you packed, Miss Lockhart?" he said frowning slightly.

"Yes, everything is ready," she said stiffly. She had heard his comment and did not think it had been meant as a compliment.

"Then I suggest you do not delay your departure as, if I am not much mistaken, we are in for a downpour and you do not want to get stuck in the mud."

Feeling as if she had been dismissed, Katherine stood. "I must thank you all for your hospitality. I only hope I can repay it in some way."

Lady Treleven rose and took her hand. "You already have, my dear. You have been a friend to Henrietta, I could not ask for more."

"I think you will find, ma'am, that she now has many more."

That young lady stepped forward and embraced Katherine. "Thank you," she said. "I am glad you are only going down the road, for I will come and see you often."

"Please do, I depend on it," Katherine said. "Please say goodbye to Lord and Lady Hayward for me, will you?"

"Of course," Henrietta said.

Lord Treleven stepped forward and bowed. "I will order your coach, Miss Lockhart."

That was all. No light-hearted compliments, no twinkle in his eyes, and no kiss of her hand. Katherine was beginning to think Miss Humphrey had been right, but perhaps the joke had started long before last night, perhaps both he and Mr Sharpe had thought it amusing to see if the bitter spinster could be brought to fall in love again. But even if that were the case, she would not fall into a decline. She was no longer an impressionable young girl, but a mature sensible woman, with far too much pride and strength to fall into the doldrums because of the pernicious behaviour of a man.

"Are you quite all right, dear?" Mrs Abbott said as the carriage drove down the main drive.

"Of course," she murmured. "I have a headache, that is all."

"It's probably the weather," Mrs Abbott said gently. "If we don't have a thunderstorm before the day is out, I will be surprised."

Mrs Abbott was not to be surprised, at least not by the thunderstorm, which did indeed break midway through the afternoon. The ladies retreated to the library as it was by far the most comfortable room in the house.

"Lord Treleven was quite right to encourage us to leave so soon," Mrs Abbott said gently as a flash of lightning brightened the room for an instant. She crossed to the window and drew the heavy curtains. "I would not have wished to be caught in this storm although I do quite enjoy sitting by the fire whilst it rages outside."

"Yes, it is very cosy," Katherine murmured absently.

The heat from the flames soon began to make her feel drowsy and her eyes had just fluttered closed, the book she had been attempting, but failing miserably to read, slipping from her fingers, when the sonorous chimes of the bell, followed swiftly by another clap of thunder made them jerk open again.

"Who on earth would come visiting in such weather?"

Mrs Abbott quickly stowed her knitting in her basket. "I cannot imagine, my dear."

They both looked up expectantly as Forster opened the door and stepped slowly into the room.

"Sir Richard Lockhart," he announced, shuffling to one side so the tall, slender gentleman behind him could gain entry. He was quite handsome in an austere, scholarly sort of fashion, with prominent cheekbones and a high sloping forehead that led to a slightly receding hairline, although he was only a few years older than his sister.

"Richard!" Katherine exclaimed, rising to her feet. "We were not expecting you!"

"I thought about sending you a letter," he said, strolling to the fire with a polite nod in Mrs Abbott's direction. He reached his hands out to the blaze. "But then I realised there was every likelihood that I would reach you before it did."

"But is aught amiss?" Katherine said.

He gave her a lopsided grin. "Does something need to be amiss for me to come and see my own sister?"

"Well, no," she conceded. "But I must admit I had not expected to see you so soon. Is Caroline with you?"

"No," he said. "She would have come but

thought better of it when I described the tedious hours she would have to while away and the state of the roads she was likely to encounter."

"I see," Katherine smiled. "You put her off. You have made a bolt for freedom. She still has the crotchets then, I take it?"

He frowned a little and glanced at Mrs Abbott.

"Oh, don't mind me, Sir Richard," she said gently. "I am sure it is quite understandable if she has."

"Yes, well, she is finding her situation a little trying," he admitted. "But that is not why I came. I wished to see for myself all these renovations, they have cost me quite a tidy sum after all. I must say this room seems very comfortable."

"Yes," agreed Katherine. "But when we arrived it was the only one, apart from the kitchen, that was."

"That bad, eh?" he said. "Come, show me around, sister."

"I will ring for some tea," Mrs Abbott said. "For I am sure you must be in need of some after your journey, Sir Richard, and perhaps a slice of cake?"

"That would be most welcome, Mrs Abbott."

Although the building had been made water-tight, and the rotten boards and windows replaced, Katherine had not been so extravagant as to order new furnishings or redecorate, apart from in the servants' quarters where two new maids had now taken up residence.

"I must say that when I got the bill I thought you had probably gone to town and expected to find a palace," Sir Richard said. "But I see that is not the case."

Katherine laughed. "When have you ever known me to be extravagant? Lord Treleven's steward Mr Hewel informed me that if the house had been left another year it would have been beyond saving! The money has gone on the fabric of the building not on luxuries I can well do without."

Her brother frowned. "I cannot say I was happy to hear we were so beholden to Treleven. I am not sure that he is a fit person for you to know."

"Oh, so now we come to it. You came because you feared I might fall in love with a wicked rake!"

"Katherine! I never thought to hear you talk in such a fashion."

"Oh, don't talk such fustian, Richard! I am hardly a green girl," she snapped, a sleepless night and the fact that his fears might prove to be quite warranted causing her loss of composure.

"If living away from my protection has caused you to talk in such a wild way, then perhaps it would be better if you returned home with me."

He looked as if would say more, but was prevented by the appearance of one of the new maids. She dropped them a curtsey and began to back out of the room.

"Rose, isn't it?" Katherine smiled at the girl.

"Yes, miss."

"There is no need for you to go, this is your room after all. We were just leaving."

Realising she had upset her very correct brother and having no wish to cause a rift between them, she took his hand as they reached the stairs.

"Forgive me, Richard, I am not quite myself, I admit. I have the headache. Mrs Abbott put it down to the thunderstorm."

He looked at her closely and appeared a little mollified. "I must say, you are looking a trifle peaky, my dear. And although you may still be green, I am well aware that you are no longer a girl and well past the age of falling in love."

"Yes, well, let us join Mrs Abbott for that cup of tea, shall we?"

His temper further improved when he inspected the shelves that spanned two walls of the library.

"I say, old Jenkins put together a fine library, I will easily be able to spend a few days in here perusing some of these books. Thank heavens he had the sense to keep this room dry at least."

Hiding a smile, his sister dutifully agreed with him.

It rained for three full days and Sir Richard soon made the library his own domain. He joined the ladies only for breakfast and dinner, but apart from that, was hardly to be seen. He had apparently stumbled upon three plays by Euripides that had not before come his way and was quite absorbed. It never once occurred to him that being smaller than the drawing room, it was far easier to heat or that the ladies might be much more comfortable there.

"I am sure I cannot blame Caroline for having the crotchets if he locks himself up all day with fusty old books," Katherine said. "He has only been here three days, and I am already nearly out of all patience with him. Whenever I try to discuss a few changes I would like to make, such as acquiring matching furniture for the drawing room, or replacing some of the sadly faded curtains, he smiles in that distracted way he has, his mind clearly upon something that happened eons ago, and murmurs whatever I think best. But I know full well that he has not heard a word I have said!"

Mrs Abbott smiled. "It is how he used to behave before he was married but he has not had so much opportunity to indulge himself since he wed. I think you will find that he looks upon his stay as a holiday and feels he can freely indulge himself without fear of reprisals."

The following day the heavens finally stopped weeping and the tedium was relieved by a visit from Lord Hayward, Belle, and Edmund.

"I could not return home without taking my leave of you," she said.

"I am so glad," Katherine smiled. "How is everyone at Elmdon?"

Belle laughed. "Busy. The weather has not deterred a stream of young gentlemen calling at the house, all delivering thank you letters from mamas I am quite sure had no idea they had such obliging sons! It is all a pretext to visit with Henrietta, of course."

"And does she seem taken with any of these gentlemen?" Mrs Abbott enquired.

"Not a one," said Belle. "I think her affections are engaged in quite another direction."

"Dr Fisher, perhaps?" Katherine said.

"Oh, undoubtedly."

"Do you think Lord Treleven would look favourably on such a match?" Mrs Abbott said gently.

Belle's forehead wrinkled in thought. "I am not sure. He seems a little out of sorts at the moment."

Edmund, who looked a little sleepy and had been quietly sitting on his mother's lap playing with the tassels on her shawl, suddenly piped up, "E's teasy as 'n' adder!"

"Edmund," Lord Hayward said a little sternly but with a laughing look at Belle. "Where on earth did you hear such language?"

The little boy was not fooled. He looked at his father and grinned. "Kenver said it."

Belle laughed. "You can hardly blame him, Hayward, when you have repeatedly taken him down to the stables over the past few days."

They did not stay long as they wanted to travel as far as they could whilst the good weather held. But as Lord Hayward took his leave of Mrs Abbott, Belle pulled Katherine to one side and said in a low voice, "I am so sorry that we have had no chance to be private for I am sure something is troubling you. I do not know what it might be, but I think I may have an inkling who may be responsible. I will only say that since you left Elmdon, Lord Treleven has not been his usual cheerful self. Whatever he may have done, or not done, if he comes calling give him the benefit of the doubt for if you trust my judgement at all, believe me when I tell you that he is not like Mr Sharpe."

She kissed Katherine's cheek and pressed a card into her hand. "Write to me and let me know how you go on, won't you?"

Soon after they had left, Sir Richard wandered into the drawing room. Mrs Abbott had gone to give Mrs Nance her recipe for bramble jelly, so he found only Katherine there, embroidering some linen.

"Hello, my dear. Forster said we had visitors. Thought I'd better show my face."

"We did," Katherine said drily. "But they have gone. They were friends who had also been staying with the Trelevens, they only came to say goodbye."

"Well in that case I'll get back to my book, if you don't mind that is?"

Katherine who had been deep in thought pondering Belle's words, assured him she did not mind at all.

~

Harry had come to respect Lord Hayward and felt some affection for his lady, however he was glad when they left. Between entertaining his guests and vetting the constant stream of silly young puppies that had come calling on his sister, he had had very little time to himself. Although not much given to introspection, he was aware of a growing feeling of dissatisfaction. Not being able to blow off steam as he would if he were in town by visiting Gentleman Jackson's boxing saloon, he decided to take Hermes for a ride and pay his overdue call on Lord Humphrey.

He was relieved when he was shown into his study without having to run the gauntlet of Miss Humphrey's simpering nonsense.

"Ah, come at last have you, Treleven. Thought you'd forgotten me," Lord Humphrey complained.

"Not at all, sir," Harry said. "I came as soon as I was able, I assure you."

"Well, sit down and explain to me if you will what is to happen to the mine now I have no partner. I read in the paper that a verdict of felo-de-se had been given – most unusual."

Without preamble Harry launched into an explanation of the outcome of the inquest.

"So we are to be partners, eh," he finally said. "You have come out of this very well, I must say."

"Indeed, I have been most fortunate, sir. I should inform you that I am just waiting for official confirmation from the lawyers and then I intend to put some major changes into effect."

"Now don't be too hasty, Treleven. What do you know about mining after all?"

"I may not know much about mining just yet, sir, but I do know how to get the best out of the people in my charge. We must do away with this token system and pay the workers a fair wage for a start," he informed him.

"Sounds more expensive," Lord Humphrey said doubtfully. "Bound to eat into the profits."

Knowing that Lord Humphrey really didn't have a clue what he was talking about, Harry patiently explained his reasoning. "I think you will find that a workforce who are treated as the skilled human beings they undoubtedly are and not like slaves who find themselves constantly indebted to their masters for the tools they use and the expensive yet poor quality food they eat, will be far more productive and thus increase the profits."

"Perhaps," he conceded.

"And I am sure it is in your interests as a magistrate and an important figure in this community to show yourself to be a benevolent and fair shareholder in the mine. Although I am sure no lasting damage to your reputation has been done by your association with Caldwell, by showing your approval of various changes I intend to make you will win over any doubters."

Lord Humphrey coloured at the mention of Caldwell. "I knew nothing of what he was about," he blustered.

"Even so," Harry said.

"What are these other changes you intend to make?"

"For a start, I intend to take on the miners from Langarne who lost their jobs."

"Well you would wouldn't you?" Lord Humphrey snorted. "They can't pay you rent if they don't have work."

"A fact you must have been well aware of when you agreed that the work should be offered to a group of foreigners," he said softly.

Lord Humphrey shifted uncomfortably in his chair. "Now, just hold on a minute. Remember I am a minority shareholder, I do not have the final say on these things."

"I have not forgotten. I intend to put my

plans into action with or without your approval but thought I would do you the courtesy of informing you of them."

"What will you do with the miners Caldwell brought in? I believe most of them are in debt to us."

"Only because Caldwell ensured they were. They have more than worked off their debt, so they will be offered a choice to stay and work side by side with our own men under the new system, or I will send them home and their so-called debts will be written off. I think you will find that most will opt for the latter option. They were here under duress, not because they wished to be. I will also be offering Doctor Fisher a fee in return for him overseeing the health of the workers."

"I'm surprised you don't offer to provide them a good hot meal every day as well!" Lord Humphrey expostulated.

"That idea is not without merit."

"It is meant to be a business not a charity," Lord Humphrey said, banging his hand on his desk. "I have a good mind to sell my share."

Harry smiled and got to his feet. "Done. Tell Boodle your terms and I will buy you out."

Harry made his way to Langarne. He had a brief word with Joe Phelps at The Anchor and asked him to spread the word that any man who wished to return to the mine would soon be able to do so.

"I will hold a meeting here next week, Joe, and explain my plans more fully if you have no objection."

"Objection, sir?" he said. "I couldn't be more pleased. Molly's increasing 'an we're going to need help we could ill afford if things had carried on as they were. I'm that grateful to you Lord Treleven, have a drink on the house."

"Congratulations, Joe, but I won't stay. There's another visit I have to pay."

He strolled over to the church and quietly let himself in through a side door that led to a small private chapel. He sat on a bench and stared down at the polished granite ledger stone that marked his father's resting place.

"The Trelevens start a new chapter, sir," he said softly. "I hope you would approve."

He was about to rise when he felt a hand on his shoulder.

"He would be proud of you," Mr Gulworthy said gently. "He always was; he often came here and said a prayer for you."

CHAPTER 16

Much to Mrs Kemp's disapproval, Harry had still not rid himself of the habit of entering Elmdon by way of the kitchen. Not only could he often find some tasty morsel to filch on his way into the main house, but he could also escape detection and discover if they had any visitors before making his presence known.

He quietly opened the door. Of Mrs Kemp there was no sign but two maids stood with their backs to him, their heads together. A few of their softly murmured words reached his ears and he stiffened. As he shut the door behind him, they broke apart and offered him a respectful curtsey. He frowned.

"Emma, isn't it?" he said, looking at the elder of the two.

"Yes, sir," she said, curtseying again and looking a little flustered.

His glance strayed to the younger one. "I don't think I know you. What is your name?"

She flushed. "Mary, sir, Mrs Kemp only took me on last week."

"Do you like working here, Mary?" he asked gently.

She nodded her head enthusiastically. "Oh, yes, milord, Ma was pleased as punch that both me and me sister got hired at the mop fair."

"Your sister works here also?"

"No, sir, she got a place over at Helagon, down the way."

Harry looked interested. "Ah, things become a little clearer. Are you aware, both of you, that gossiping about your betters could get you dismissed?"

"Oh, we weren't—"

"Then why did I hear Miss Lockhart's name on your lips when I opened the door?"

He looked at them sternly and they dropped their heads in shame.

"Mary?" The word was softly spoken but brought the girl's head up. Her eyes were bright and tears threatened to spill over onto her flushed cheeks.

"Oh, don't turn me off, sir," she pleaded, twisting her hands in her apron. "We needs the money. I wasn't saying anything nasty, only that Rose – that's me sister – said as how Miss Lockhart's brother had come to stay, turned up in that nasty storm and she heard him being out of reason cross with her and sayin' as how he would take her back home. She only told me 'cos she were worried, sir. If miss goes away, Rose might lose her job."

Something in her master's face made her gasp and then the tears began to flow.

"Please, sir," she sobbed.

Harry's gaze gentled. "There's no need to cry," he said. "I have no intention of having you turned off. Now I suggest you get back to work. If Mrs Kemp sees you being idle she'll certainly have something to say."

He went straight to his study, paced up and down for a few moments, crossed to the brandy decanter, removed the stopper, held it for a moment and then replaced it. Turning on his heel he retraced his steps through the kitchen and went to the stables. The vague, nagging feeling of dissatisfaction that had plagued him the past few days had now crystallised into a feeling of loss, an emptiness he had not experienced before. If he had been in any doubt as to the cause of this malady, he was no longer. He strode up and down impatiently as he waited for Kenver to bring Hermes out to him.

The horse's nostrils flared and his tail twitched as he swung up into the saddle.

"I'm not sure you should take him out again, sir," Kenver said. "You're as twitchy as a toad on a hot shovel and he knows it."

"When I want your opinion, Kenver, I'll ask for it."

Kenver whistled and a slow grin crossed his face as he watched him race out of the yard. He might have his mother's colouring but the disdainful look he had thrown at him and his unusually sharp manner, were all his father.

Katherine picked up her embroidery and then sat unmoving, staring into space for some time. Eventually she sighed and put it down again. She went up to her room and donned an old bonnet and a warm pelisse and went for a turn about the garden. It was now a blank canvas, a little like her life, she realised. She had been nowhere, done nothing of any import. Was she really content to dwindle into an old maid in this little backwater? Might it not be better to return with her brother and try to coax Caroline out of her sullens? That she made him uncomfortable she was sure. He certainly seemed in no hurry to return to her.

She came to the small cherub fountain. A gentle smile curved her lips as she thought of her companion. How disappointed Mrs Abbott would be if they left before she had the chance to see her plans for the garden come to fruition. No, she would stay until next summer at least. Richard had chosen his own bride after all. She did not wish to find herself in the middle of their dissatisfaction and they were far more likely to find a way to make each other comfortable without her interference.

She turned and began to meander back towards the house her eyes rising to survey the newly mended roof. It was easy to see where the repair had been made for the newly laid slate tiles gleamed brighter than all the rest. She came to a halt and a wide slow smile curved her generous lips, an inkling of an idea beginning to take hold. Perhaps there was something useful she could do here.

"Miss Lockhart."

Her eyes fell and her smile slipped. Lord

Treleven strode around the corner of the house purposefully.

"John told me I would find you here."

Her heart started to beat a little faster as she registered the intensity of his gaze.

"I wish you would smile for me," he said softly.

"I cannot imagine why," she said coolly. "There is no one here to witness your success after all."

His brows snapped together. "What the devil do you mean by that?"

She suddenly felt uncertain of her ground. It was much easier to suspect him of enjoying himself at her expense in his absence. But when he stood before her, she was reminded that the vitality and energy which characterised him, his love of life and openness of manner, all spoke against his being capable of any sort of maliciousness towards her. She remembered Belle's advice and took a steadying breath. "I am not sure. Forget I said it. I am out of sorts."

"Walk with me," he said, still frowning.

A heavy silence hung between them and she sought in vain for a way to break it. They both started to speak at the same time and then broke off, this encounter attended by a constraint and awkwardness that had never before marked their dealings with each other. At least not on both sides.

After a moment he said, "I am glad to find you here, I had heard that your brother had come to visit and was afraid he might have whisked you away."

Katherine gave him a sideways glance, her brow furrowed. "You run too deep for me, sir," she finally said. "Your words imply that you would not wish for such an event yet only a few days ago you could not hurry me out of your house fast enough."

His smiled ruefully. "I did not wish for you to be caught in the storm, I—" he hesitated, "I needed some room to think."

"Does not Elmdon have enough rooms for you to think in?"

He took a few quick strides away from her, jerked to a stop, swivelled and returned. He took both her hands in a firm grip, his eyes burning bright. "It would not matter if it had a thousand rooms, for if I knew you to be in just one, it is to that room that I would be drawn."

He spoke with such tortured sincerity that she could not doubt the veracity of his words. Her heart trembled and her lips parted on a soft gasp. His eyes fell to them for a moment.

"Would that have been so terrible?" she whispered.

"I did not wish to hurt you," he said softly. "I had to be sure of my own heart before I could even attempt to find a place in yours."

"And you are sure now?" she murmured, her eyes searching his, hardly daring to believe that her own feelings might be returned.

He stepped closer until only a breath separated them. "I am not a romantic man," he murmured. "I had never met a woman who could hold my interest, I doubted such a one existed. But when I was away you filled my thoughts, I could not wait to return to you. I liked knowing you were under my roof. When you were there no longer, I felt your absence and could not be comfortable. There was an emptiness," he took her hand and pressed it against his heart, "here."

"I felt it too," she said, her voice catching.

"Kate," he groaned, "my Kate, my love."

The possessive way he uttered the words stopped her breath. He dipped his head and pressed his lips to hers and she was lost. Light and longing flooding her, she swayed and he caught her to him fiercely, parting her lips and deepening his kiss. The shock of his tongue sliding over hers sent pulses of tingling pleasure spiralling to all her hidden places. When his mouth finally lifted from her own, she whimpered, feeling the loss, then sighed as he trailed the lightest butterfly kisses along her jawline before gently sucking on her delicate lobe.

"Harry, Harry," she moaned.

"Treleven! Step away from my sister!"

She chuckled and said softly, "Now we are in the suds – my bookish brother thinks you a wicked rake."

"Is his opinion important to you?" Harry murmured.

"I would not wish him to be unhappy."

"Then I shall have to convince him that his beautiful sister has reformed me."

"And have I?" Katherine asked, a hint of vulnerability and uncertainty in her eyes.

Harry stepped back and bowed low over her hand, brushing his lips against it.

"Never doubt it, Kate."

"I knew you should never have stayed beneath his roof," Sir Richard said, closing the distance between them. "Just look what comes of it. Have you no honour, sir?"

"Lockhart," Harry offered him a small bow. "I hope I have my fair share of it."

"But you were kissing my sister, sir," he protested.

"Yes," he acknowledged, his eyes twinkling. "But I can assure you I did not when she was beneath my roof."

"That does not make it any better! You should not be kissing her at all!"

His eyes raked his sister. "I did not see you putting up much of a struggle, Katherine. What possessed you? I would never have believed you capable of displaying such loose morals and poor judgement."

She smiled gently at her brother. "It would appear I am not past the age of falling in love, after all."

"Climb down from your high horse, Lockhart," Harry said, unwilling to have his love the target of such disapproval for long. "Do not tell me you did not kiss your wife before you married her? Despite your sister's poor judgement and loose morals, I have every intention of making an honest woman of her."

He glanced down at her, his gaze warm. "As soon as possible."

"Oh, you have, eh? Is this what you want, Katherine?"

She took her brother's hands and squeezed them.

"Yes, there is nothing I want more." Her cheeks were flushed and her eyes shone with such radiant happiness that Sir Richard was left with very little to say.

He glanced at Harry. "Well, you'd better come into the house, Treleven, we need to discuss a few things."

Harry grinned. "Certainly, old chap. Give me a few moments first though, will you?"

"Oh, very well," Sir Richard said. "You'll find me in the library."

Harry led Katherine behind a nearby tree. He leant against it and pulled her hard against him claiming her mouth in another long, lingering kiss.

"Your brother is right," he murmured. "You are quite abandoned, and to think I thought you old-cattish when we first met."

She opened her mouth to utter a scathing response but he covered it again with his.

"What were you smiling at when I came into the garden," he asked her as they slowly dawdled back towards the house.

"The slates," she murmured. "They had given me an idea I hope you will approve of."

"Go on."

"I think we should start a school for the miners' children."

He took her hand and raised it to his lips. "I do approve. I had already intended to improve conditions as much as possible but I had not, I admit, thought of that. It is an excellent idea."

She beamed at him. "I want to feel I have made a difference in some small way."

He looked at her with admiration. "You have already made a difference, to Henrietta and to me."

"Oh, I do not think I can take all the credit for Henrietta's transformation. You do know that she is well on the way to being in love with Doctor Fisher? Do you approve?"

Harry smiled down at her. "He is a good man from a good family. I think he will make his mark upon the world. If she is of the same mind six months from now, I will not object. Now, my dear, perhaps you will explain your earlier comment about my needing an audience."

She coloured and told him of her conversation with Miss Humphrey.

"I did not believe it in my heart," she assured him.

He drew her to him for an instant. "It is understandable that you should doubt. I know your history with Sharpe because I forced it out of him."

"Oh, how did you do that?" she said interested.

"I strangled him."

Katherine chuckled. "Your methods are a little crude, sir."

He grinned. "But effective. When we are married—"

"I know you are not romantic," she interrupted him gently. "But even though I may be old-cattish, I find that I am. Would you mind very much asking me?"

He laughed down at her and then framing her face with his hands, he gently stroked her soft cheek with his thumb and looked deeply into her eyes.

"Will you marry me as soon as it may be arranged, sweet Kate?"

"Yes, yes, dear love," she replied sighing. "I will."

THE END

Thank you for reading Katherine!

Thank you for your support! I do hope you have enjoyed reading Katherine. If you would consider leaving a short review on Amazon, I would be very grateful. It really helps readers know what to expect, and helps raise my profile, which as a relatively new author is so very helpful.

I love to hear from my readers and can be contacted at: jenny@jennyhambly.com

Other books in the series

Belle – Bachelor Brides 0
Rosalind – Bachelor Brides 1
Sophie – Bachelor Brides 2
Katherine – Bachelor Brides 3

Belle is available, free, to anyone who joins my mailing list at: https://jennyhambly.com/book/belle-2/

ABOUT THE AUTHOR

I love history and the Regency period in particular. I grew up on a diet of Jane Austen, Charlotte and Emily Bronte, and Georgette Heyer. Later I put my love of reading to good use and gained a 1st class honours degree in literature.

I now write traditional Regency romance novels. I like to think my characters, though flawed, are likeable, strong, and true to the period. I have thoroughly enjoyed writing my Bachelor Brides series. Writing has always been my dream and I am fortunate enough to have been able to realise that dream.

I live by the sea in Plymouth, England, with my partner, Dave. I like reading, sailing, wine, getting up early to watch the sunrise in summer, and long quiet evenings by the wood burner in our cabin on the cliffs in Cornwall in winter.

facebook.com/AuthorJennyHambly

twitter.com/hambly_jenny

Printed in Great Britain
by Amazon

13584590R00182